Case of the Stolen Art V. ____
A Lorelei Silence Mystery

By
Karen Stillwagon

Edited by
Kelsea Koths

This is a work of fiction. Names, characters, places, and incidents are either the product of the author's imagination or are used fictitiously, and any resemblance to actual persons, living or dead, business establishments, event or locales in entirely coincidental.
Karen Stillwagon

First Edition September 2019

For my Family

1

The little dog ran down the beach, chasing the gulls near the water. As the gulls took flight, the little dog chased the waves, barking at the foam. A storm was off to the West. Black clouds could be seen near the horizon, building up for a strong storm. The gulls came back to rest in the sand while little dog looped around for another go at them near the end of the cove.

"Bindi, come!" the young woman called, stopping the little dog in her tracks. She turned to look at her person before she continued to chase birds.

The woman, with wisps of long curly red hair blowing in the wind, called again, "Bindi!" She tried tucking the loose strands back up in her messy bun but was unsuccessful.

The little dog stopped again but didn't look back this time. She started barking at a log that had washed up at the base of the cliff. The young woman finally reached the little dog, leaned down, and hooked the red plaid leash to the dog's harness of the same design.

"What has you so excited?" the young woman asked as she pulled the little terrier to her. She looked at the log and saw the shape of a person crumpled behind it. She looked close, saw it was an elderly woman, her pale skin visible from under the tangles of long silver hair. The young woman reached down, and gently placed her fingers on the neck of the old woman, felt for a pulse. A hand grasped the young woman's wrist in a weak grip. The young woman gasped.

"Help me." The voice came like a whisper from the wind, the sound of the waves almost drowning it out.

"I'm going to help you," the young woman said gently as she loosened the old woman's grip on her wrist. She took off her sweatshirt and placed it over the old woman, hoping to keep her warm until she could make it back with help.

"Bindi, stay." The wire haired fox terrier was sniffing the old woman. She looked up and kept her eyes on her person.

"Please," the old woman whispered, "don't leave me."

"I'm going to leave Bindi here with you, I need to get up on the cliffs to see if I can get cell reception." The young woman then knelt down, placed the back of her hand on the older woman's cheek, brushing away the tangled hair until she could see the old woman's wet eyes. "My name is Lorelei, I am not leaving you but I need to get help. I cannot move you without fear of hurting you any more than you already are."

A single tear ran down the old woman's cheek as she nodded.

"I know Bindi doesn't seem like much, but she's loyal and will keep you safe."

Lorelei headed back down the beach, toward the trail she and Bindi had come down just a few minutes before.

The trail was well used by the surfers in the area, making it easy to climb back up. She had to use some of the branches that hung over the trail to help her since she couldn't calm her breathing.

Once she made her way to the top, she pulled out her phone and checked for service. Still no bars. She headed toward the closest house on the dead end road. She knocked hard and waited a minute. No answer so she went to the next house where two cars were parked in the driveway. Lorelei pounded on the door until a woman answered. After explaining what had happened, the woman led her to the phone where Lorelei promptly called 911.

"I found a woman injured on the beach, in the cove at Lighthouse Way. I was walking my dog on the beach and found her. She is alive, I left her covered with my sweatshirt. You need to send the paramedics down the trail." Lorelei listened to the 911 dispatch operator for a moment and answered, "I can't wait for the police, I promised her I would be back. I will be with her when someone shows up." She hung up the phone, thanked the woman, then headed back toward the trail that led back to the cove.

Once she made it down the trail Bindi started barking but did not leave the old woman's side.

"Good girl," Lorelei said as she sat next to the old woman. Bindi climbed into her lap and calmed down,

"Thank you," the old woman said.

"For what?"

"For coming back."

"I told you I wasn't going to leave you, I just had to call for help." She took the woman's cold hand into hers and held it tight. "Can you tell me your name?" Lorelei asked.

"Dee, Dee Brown," she whispered as she reached for Bindi with her other hand. She dug her fingers into Bindi's wiry fur, petting her. Bindi stayed close to Dee as she tried to stay on Lorelei's lap. The little terrier licked Dee's hand.

"What happened?" Lorelei asked.

She turned her head away from Lorelei and stared out at the waves breaking on the ocean. Some sandpipers were played in the waves, running up and down as the water chased them.

"Bindi was chasing the gulls when she found you," Lorelei said, trying to keep Dee talking.

"I'm watching a friend's house. I was walking around the yard when I slipped and fell down the cliff." Her eyes didn't meet Lorelei's. Dee kept looking everywhere but at her. Lorelei felt a chill run down her spine.

"You're lucky," Lorelei said, not knowing what else to say.

"I am lucky you found me," Dee said. She closed her eyes and said nothing else.

Lorelei stayed next to her, hugging Bindi, and holding Dee's hand as she waited for someone to come relieve her.

Lorelei heard sirens off in the distance. They grew louder as they drew near, then went silent. Lorelei didn't know how long it would take them to find her.

"I'm going to leave you for a few minutes again," she said to Dee, "I'm going to wait for the paramedics at the trail head."

"Okay," Dee's voice was just above a whisper.

"I'll leave Bindi with you," Lorelei said.

"Thank you," Dee responded as Lorelei placed Bindi's leash in the hand she had been holding.

"She won't leave you, but hold the leash just in case," Lorelei said. "I won't be far and I won't be gone long."

Lorelei headed back to the trail while Bindi, without a sound, guarded Dee. It always pulled at Lorelei's heartstrings to ask Bindi to do something that meant leaving her, but Bindi always pulled though and was a better dog for it. Whether it made Lorelei a better person, leaving her best friend, her companion who trusted her, she didn't think so.

Voices sounded at the top of the trailhead. Lorelei waved for them to come down to the cove.

"We got a call of a woman needing help," one of the paramedics said as he reached Lorelei.

"Yes. She's over there," Lorelei said as she pointed down

the beach. "I found her when I was walking my dog earlier." The paramedic made his way toward Dee Brown, carrying a large case, without waiting for his partner, who was just starting down the trail.

Bindi barked as he got close.

"It's okay, fella," he said as he approached.

"Her name is Bindi," Lorelei said as she caught up to him. "It's okay honey," Lorelei said to the little terrier, calming her down.

The old woman grabbed the little dog's leash and pulled her close.

"It's okay," Lorelei said as she sat down in the sand, "I have a paramedic here with me."

Dee released her grip on the little dog as the man approached.

"Can you tell me what happened?" he asked as he set his bag next to her.

"I was checking on a friend's house. She and her husband are gone for the month. When I checked the yard, I stumbled and fell. I didn't have anything to grab hold of so I slid down the cliff."

"What is your name?" he asked as he started pulling instruments out of his bag.

"My name is Dee Brown. I live across the street. I was watching my neighbor's home while they are away," she repeated. Lorelei wanted to interrupt, worried the old woman hit her head since she kept repeating herself. But she waited to see how the old woman would continue.

"Where do they live?" he asked as he checked her vital signs.

"There," she said, motioning to the home straight above them.

"So you were checking on their home?" he asked.

"Yes. And their home was fine. I went out the back and

walked the back yard. I'm guessing the rain the last few days made the ground soft. I slipped and fell."

"And no one was near?" he asked.

"No." She kept her head turned from the paramedic.

"And I found her, about a half hour ago. I called as soon as I could get someone to answer their door." Lorelei looked down at Dee and wondered if she could have helped her sooner.

"Answer their door?" the paramedic asked.

"Yes," Lorelei answered. "I knocked on a few door before someone would respond. The cell phone reception is terrible here."

"Ms. Brown, my name is Alan Rowe, and I'm going to take this sweatshirt off you and look for injuries." Lorelei took the sweatshirt from him and pulled it back on, hoping to avoid more chills. Bindi crawled into her lap but did not relax. Her little body shivered as she kept an eye on the man working on the woman she was supposed to be guarding.

Lorelei turned away, trying to give them privacy as Alan Rowe examined Dee Brown. The tide was going out and the roar of the waves seemed more distant.

Bindi let out a low growl. When Lorelei looked over she saw that the other paramedic was approaching. She was a petite woman with short dark curly hair, who handled another large case with ease. Lorelei put her arms around Bindi, whispering in her ear to help calm her down.

"We aren't going to be able to get her out of here by stretcher," the woman said. "Want me to call for an airlift?"

"Ms. Brown, this is my partner Cathrine McClain, but you can call her Cat." Turning to his partner he continued, "I think we can get her out of here. Her vitals are good, she's moving around, reflexes are good. We need a stretcher and rope. Cops should be here any minute and aide us if we need help." He turned to Lorelei, "Ma'am, can I get your information?"

"Lorelei Silence, I am staying at the Charleston Harbor Inn, right in town."

"Are you just passing through?" Alan asked as he took down her information.

"No, I just moved back to town a few days ago, after being gone for a number of years. I inherited my grandparents home, you can't see it from here, but it's right up there, before you turn onto Lighthouse Way." She was rambling too, but couldn't help herself.

Alan Rowe kept writing, "And your phone number?"

Lorelei gave him her cell number.

"Do you have a work number, in case the police want to talk to you?"

"Police?" she asked.

"I'm surprised they aren't here yet, they come out with these calls, as does the fire department. We should be hearing more sirens." And as he finished writing, Lorelei could more hear sirens in the distance again.

"I'll go meet them." Cat McClain jogged back down the beach to the trail.

"I don't want to be carried out on a stretcher," Dee said after a moment.

"It will be safest," Alan Rowe told her as he pulled a foil blanket from his case to cover her up.

"I'm pretty sure I could walk, with help maybe?"

"I don't think so." He was making her as comfortable as he could while he waited for his partner to come back.

"Do you still need me?" Lorelei asked.

"You aren't leaving, are you?" Dee reached up for Lorelei's hand. Lorelei leaned over and took it in her own hand.

"I will find out where you are being taken and I'll be there before you arrive," Lorelei reassured her, "I need to take Bindi home and change." She looked down at her sweats which were covered with sand and seaweed.

"She'll be taken to Bay Area Hospital." Alan Rowe said. He did not look up at Lorelei, he kept working on Dee. "And please talk to the cops before you leave, let them know what happened."

"I can do that. Dee, I will be there when you get there. Is there anyone I can call for you?" Lorelei said.

"No, my husband passed a few years ago. It's just me and my dog."

"Okay," Lorelei started to stand.

"Wait!" Dee started again, "Can you go to my house and lock it up for me? My dog is in the back yard. Can you put her inside for me? She's not used to being left out."

"Which house is yours?"

"It's the large green one across the main road, all windows upstairs. There is a large garage with an apartment built on top of it, less than a quarter mile from the trail head, on the right. You can't miss it." Dee said, her voice getting stronger with each sentence.

"I'll check on it and lock it up for you. I am assuming you have keys to get back in?" This brought a smile to Dee's lips, making Lorelei think she was younger than what she had originally thought.

"Oh don't you worry about that, I'll be fine." Lorelei took that smile with her as she made for her escape.

The police were heading down the beach, led by Cat McClain.

"This is the lady who found the injured woman," Cat said as she approached Lorelei, who kept Bindi's leash tight to her side to keep the little dog from jumping.

"I'm Officer Holloway, and this is my partner Officer Smith," the tall dark-haired cop said as she stopped in front of Lorelei, blocking her way to the trail.

Officer Smith pulled a small notebook from the breast

pocket of his uniform, opened it, and started writing. "Can you tell us what happened?"

"Bindi and I were walking on the beach when we found the old woman," Lorelei said.

"And Bindi is?" Smith asked as he continued to write.

"My dog," she said. Bindi's ears perked up at her name and looked up at her person. "She was chasing the gulls down the beach. When she got near the log she stopped and started barking. When I called her she wouldn't come back. When I went to get her, I found her next to the lady who was lying there. She was cold, scared, and didn't want me to leave. I left Bindi with her and ran to get help."

"Where did you go?" Smith asked. His blond hair was long on the top, with the sides cut short. He kept sweeping his hair out of his face as the wind swirled around inside the cove.

"I climbed back up the trail, couldn't get cell reception, so I knocked on doors until someone opened up and let me use their phone." Lorelei bent over and picked up Bindi, holding her close to her chest.

"Which houses?" he asked.

"The one to the right, when you get to the road, but no one was home. The next house, to the right, had cars in the driveway so I thought someone would be there, and a woman let me in to use the phone."

"Okay, can I get your name, address, and phone number in case we have more questions for you," Officer Smith said.

Lorelei rattled off the same information she had given the paramedic and Officer Smith wrote it down in his notebook.

"If there isn't anything else, I would like to go and get cleaned up so I can meet Dee at the hospital," Lorelei said.

"Okay, we will be in touch if we need any further information." Officer Smith closed his notebook and headed off down the beach where Dee Brown was still on the ground.

Lorelei climbed back up the trail, making it the top in

record time, with Bindi pulling her the entire way. She wanted to get out of there before anyone had more questions for her.

Another cop car came and parked behind the police cruiser that was already there. The EMT's had blocked a driveway on the dead end road. The two officers didn't look at Lorelei as she unlocked her Honda. Her thoughts strayed to the fact that she would have to get a new car soon. Yes, this car had taken her through high school and college, but she needed something she wouldn't be embarrassed to drive.

After starting her car, she did a u-turn and headed back to Charleston. Dee's house, which was only about a hundred yards up the road. As Lorelei pulled into the driveway, a firetruck passed her and turned onto Lighthouse Way. She nosed her car close to the garage.

"You gotta wait here," she told Bindi as she ruffled her fur. "I don't know if her dog would welcome your sassy little self."

Lorelei made her way to the gate and let herself in. She was greeted by a sweet golden retriever who seemed glad to have company, even if she didn't know who it was.

"How're you doing?" She knelt down and rubbed the dog's ears while avoiding the tongue that kept trying to lick her. She found the collar and a name tag. "Hi Lily, I'm a friend of your momma's and she asked me to let you inside the house. She didn't want you outside by yourself." She stood and Lily followed her to the back door. When Lorelei opened it, Lily went to her large bed at the bottom of the stairs, and after making a few circles, making sure it was comfortable, she plopped down.

Before Lorelei left, she noticed a set of keys sitting on the small table next to the door. Without thinking, she picked them up and pocketed them before locking the door. She walked around the back yard, which was secured by a tall wooden fence. The lawn was mowed, the leaves raked, and there was a chicken coop that was well taken care of. To her left was the back of the garage, and a flight of steps leading up to the apartment Dee had mentioned. She left back through the gate, got in her car and left.

Once back at the Charleston Harbor Inn, Lorelei and Bindi ran upstairs. Bindi went straight for her food and fresh water. Lorelei stripped, leaving a trail of clothes behind her as she made her way to the shower. She did not want to show up at the hospital all wind blown, sandy, and wet, as she struggled getting out of her sweat pants.

Once clean, she dressed in Levi's and a sweater, pulled on her boots and went in search for her hairbrush. She was torn between getting her long red curls cut off into something fashionable or just keep tossing it up in a messy bun. She found the brush with her hair dryer. After letting out a long sigh, she resigned herself to blow drying her hair. It would take a bit more time, but if she was going to keep it long, she needed to remember it was high maintenance.

Lorelei leaned out the bathroom door, checking the clock on the living room wall. She'd been home for almost an hour. She had not heard any more sirens, but she didn't know if they would use them while taking Dee to the hospital, or, if they had, she wouldn't have heard them while in the shower. She left her hair half damp, pulled it back up into a messy bun and ran for the door. Bindi followed.

"You're staying home this time," she said as she caught Bindi in mid jump. "Protect the fort!" She tossed Bindi down before grabbing a squeaky toy to throw for her. She then reached for the sweats that lay on the front room floor where she had left them, and pulled out the keys she took from Dee's house. She locked up and headed down to her car. As she unlocked her Honda she tried to remember the way to the hospital.

2

Officers Smith and Holloway watched the paramedics and the firemen hoist Dee Brown up the well worn trail on a stretcher. Officer Smith offered to help but was told that too many would make the task that much more difficult, so he left them to carry her up to the waiting ambulance.

"What are your thoughts on this one?" Officer Smith asked as they were alone on the beach.

"I think we need to go up there and look around," Officer Holloway said, turning to her partner. "I think something happened up there that either frightened her, or bothered her enough to run, but not for help."

"Yeah, something isn't right," Officer Smith said as he started making his way back to where Dee Brown slid down the embankment.   Craning his neck, he looked up the hundred feet Dee had come down, seeing freshly disturbed dirt. "I'm going to guess she came down feet first, those ruts look like heel marks to me. And she's lucky she came down where she did since it's slightly sloped. If she'd been ten feet on either side, she would have come straight down, broken herself up good, if she survived at all."

"It looks like this washed out a while ago. I don't know

why anyone would want a home so close to the cliffs the way these banks are eroding," Officer Holloway said, looking around the cove's walls.

"Let's have a look from above," Officer Smith said and they walked south, back toward the trail.

The large house sat away from the bluff but still had a magnificent view, unobstructed by trees. There was a well-worn path that went along the bluff, in front of the properties, connecting all the homes along the way. Officer Holloway walked around the house, looking for signs of a break in, or anything out of the ordinary that would frighten Dee Brown. She could see nothing out of place, no open doors, no broken windows.

"Here's where she went down," Officer Smith called to her, "and there seems to be foot prints on top of hers."

Officer Holloway made her way back around the house and found the foot path that lead to her partner.

"You can see where she tripped," Smith said, pointing to an exposed root, "and when she fell, she went right over the edge. That must be what she was able to hang on to, to stop her from sliding all the way down at once." He pointed to another exposed root, a quarter of the way down the slope. "And here are another set of footprints, over hers, that had stopped here, and the person was either looking at the view, and not seeing Dee Brown hanging on for dear life, or it was just one of the home owners walking along who stopped to admire the view, and didn't see Dee Brown, lying in a heap at the bottom of the bluff."

"You'd need to lean over pretty far to see where she was," Holloway said, "and by where these tracks are, they could not see her on the beach."

"But they would see her hanging onto that root," Smith

said.

"Do you think she was pushed?" Holloway asked.

"I'm not sure what to think at the moment. She's scared and she's hiding things. We need to get to the hospital and question her again, let her know she's safe talking to us, and maybe we can get some answers."

They arrived at the hospital only to find Dee Brown unavailable. She was down in X-ray but the paramedics who brought her in were standing in the hallway next to her room.

"Alan, Cat," Officer Michael Smith started, "how was Ms. Brown on the way in?"

"Hey Michael," Cat said, "funny you should ask that. She was protesting a bit too much, just kept saying she was fine and she wanted to go home. I told her she was lucky to be alive after falling down the bluff the way she did."

"Did she tell you anymore about what happened?" Amy asked.

"Nothing," Alan said, "but as we were looking her over, before she was taken out of the cove, she kept looking up, like she was waiting for someone up there, but as far as I could tell, there was no one there."

"I didn't see anything up there either," Cat said.

"We are going to stick around, have a talk with Dee Brown again, and see if we can't get some answers," Amy said.

"Good luck," said Alan before he and Cat made their way down the hallway, and out of the Emergency Room.

"How do you want to handle this?" Amy asked Michael.

Going though his notes, Micheal said, "I remember the woman on the beach, Lorelei Silence, telling me Dee Brown was afraid and didn't want to be left alone. She left her little dog with her while she ran for help."

"I wouldn't want to be left alone either," Amy said, "especially if I had just slid down that bluff."

"But you would want help, wouldn't you? Wouldn't you hope the person who found you would be able to get you the help you needed?" Michael asked.

"I see your point, but Ms. Brown may have been in shock, or was confused."

"She had her faculties about her when we arrived, but we don't know her mindset when Lorelei found her."

Amy looked quizzically at her partner at the informal mention of the witness's name. Michael was still looking at his notes, a hint of a smile crossing his lips. Amy didn't care for the smile, it was unbecoming of Michael to smile at a witness's name.

"Michael," Amy warned, "we don't need you screwing things up because the witness is a cute red head. We have to keep a clear head and find out what happened."

"Excuse me?" Michael did look up from his notebook this time.

"When you call a witness by her first name with that smile on your face, I see potential for a disaster in the making."

"I'm not pulling a Rossi here by dating the witness, or the coworkers, or anyone else he manages to fancy that day," Michael said, his cheeks flushed, "and I will not be doing anything that could be considered inappropriate that will put the defense on high alert." Officer Rossi had been a member of the police department until their Captain found Rossi in a compromising position with a witness.

"If you say so," Amy laughed. She never knew her partner to act on his emotions when dealing with a witness. His gut feelings, which were usually spot on, were another story, and she was sure his gut was telling him something was off on this one. She felt it too. Dee Brown was not telling them the whole story.

"Excuse me," the technician said as he wheeled Dee Brown, in her bed past the officers, back into her cubicle in the emergency room. Both Michael and Amy stepped to the side so the tech could maneuver the bed back into position and get Dee set back on her machines.

After the technician left, Michael Smith and Amy Holloway went back in to talk to Dee Brown.

"I don't know what more I can tell you," Dee said after listening to Officer Holloway ask again if there was something else Dee remembered. "I tripped over a root and slid down the bluff."

"Ms. Brown, we noticed foot prints over the top of yours from where you slipped. Did you see anyone above, after you had fallen?" Officer Smith asked.

"No, but it's a trail that is used often by people, and I couldn't see the trail from where I landed. And if I did see someone, you can bet I would have called for help." Dee stared at Officer Smith for a moment before breaking eye contact and looking away again.

"Okay," he said, closing up his notebook and putting it back the breast pocket of his uniform.

They stepped out of the curtained room Dee Brown was in and walked down the hallway, out of earshot.

"She's hiding something, but until we can get her to talk to us, we have nothing to go on," Michael said.

"I agree," Amy said, "we are just going to have to wait until she's ready to open up and tell us what she saw. We can't force her to talk. We need to leave her our cards and hope she will come forward."

3

Lorelei parked and ran into the Emergency Room. She went to the admission desk to get information.

"I am here with the woman who was brought in, the woman found at the beach."

"Slow down," the elderly woman behind the partition said.

"Dee Brown," Lorelei said, taking a deep breath, "she was brought in not long ago, I would like to know if I can go back and sit with her."

"Just a moment, please." The woman called back to the ER nurse station. "Hello, yes, I have…" she looked at Lorelei with raised eyebrows.

"Lorelei." She let her name hang in the air.

Back into the phone she said, "I have Lorelei here to see Ms. Brown. Yes,… okay, I'll send her back." She hung up and pointed to the big double doors that started to open. "Through there and you want number twelve."

"Thank you!" Lorelei made her way into the emergency room and started looking for numbers above the closed curtains for each room. She turned back to head back up the hallway and nearly ran into the cops from the beach.

"I'm trying to find Dee Brown's room"

"This way," Officer Smith said, leading her down the hallway.

"I told her I would be here before she arrived and I am late. I had to get cleaned up." She could feel her cheeks flush as Officer Smith turned to look at her.

Officer Holloway gave her a small smile. "You're here now, no need to worry. I am guessing the doctor is still with her so she won't know that you're late."

"I just wanted to get to her before she got worried."

Smith led her past the nurses station and to the corner room. He pulled back the curtain and said, "Ms. Brown, your friend is here."

Dee's soft blue eyes lit up at the sight of Lorelei. She reached up, searching for her hand, a hospital band hung loosely around her wrist. Lorelei reached for her and held tight.

"Your hands are much warmer than they were before," she laughed.

"I thought you weren't going to make it," Dee whispered to her, looking past her to Smith and Holloway.

"I told you I'd be here. I had to get changed and cleaned up so they would let me in to see you. I didn't think I'd be taken seriously if I showed up in beach clothes."

"This is a fishing community, honey, people will be here dressed much worse," Dee said.

Dee finally looked at the police who had come in with her.

"Ms. Brown, where are the people who's house you were checking on?"

"Paris, visiting their first great grand baby, and I've been feeding their cat."

"I just need to make sure we have everything." He turned to Lorelei. "And can you remember anything else, see anything out of the ordinary?"

"I wouldn't know what is ordinary since I just moved back

to the area. It was only my second time down to that cove." Lorelei squeezed Dee's hand.

"So you aren't from around here?" he asked.

"My family moved from the area about sixteen years ago. My grandparents passed away a few months ago, and I just recently found out they left me their house."

The cop looked down at his notebook for a moment. A smile briefly reached his lips before saying, "Where are you staying again?"

"I'm staying at the Charleston Harbor Inn, have been there a few days." Lorelei wondered why he needed this information.

"Please don't go too far, we may have more questions for you." He closed his notebook.

"I'm not going anywhere. I'm going to stay with Dee until she's either in a room or released."

The curtain was pulled back and a man walked in. He was older, with salt and pepper hair, wearing a white coat. "I'm Dr. Jamison, and I'm afraid I don't know when we will be releasing Ms. Brown. We are waiting for some test results to come back."

"I told you I feel fine, just a little sore from sliding down the bluff and embarrassed for needing to be brought in by ambulance." Dee sat herself up in bed.

"Your vitals are fine, I am waiting for the X-rays, to know if there is any injuries we can't see," Dr. Jamison told her.

"How long will that be?" Lorelei asked.

"We should have them anytime. Are you sure you want to go home tonight?" Dr. Jamison asked Dee.

"I would do much better if I could sleep in my own bed," she replied.

The cops left the room. The doctor started to leave but turned back to Dee. "Do you have anyone staying with you?"

"I'll be staying with her," Lorelei said before Dee could

respond.

"Okay, then I'll be back as soon as I have some answers." He left, pulling the curtain closed behind him.

"Would you be okay with me staying with you?" Lorelei asked Dee once they were alone.

"I would appreciate you staying, I don't want to be alone, and I really don't want to stay here any longer than I have to." Dee turned her head from Lorelei, and let out the deep breath she'd been holding in.

"What are you not telling the police?" Lorelei asked as she pulled a chair close to Dee and sat down. She grabbed her hand again and held it tight.

"I don't know what you're talking about," Dee whispered as she kept her face turned away from Lorelei.

They sat in silence for a moment.

"Were you able to put my dog inside and lock my house?" Dee finally asked, breaking the silence.

"I did, and I grabbed the keys off the small table in the foyer. I didn't know if you had keys with you and didn't want you locked out of your house." Lorelei realized she was rubbing the back of Dee's hand, trying to comfort her.

"I have a key hidden outside my house, I've locked myself out one too many times not to have a hidden key."

"Okay, I'll get your keys back to you once you're home."

"I'd appreciate you keeping a set of keys," Dee said.

"As much as I can understand that, you really don't know me. For all you know I am a fugitive running from the law and using you as a way to hide out."

Dee let out a laugh, "Yes, and I am on the FBI's ten most wanted."

Lorelei laughed at this. "You and I will do well together."

"You look just like your mom," Dee said after a few more moments of silence.

"You know my mom?" Lorelei tried to picture the

woman's face, but couldn't.

"I didn't recognize you at first, I haven't seen you in quite some time."

"I'm sorry, I don't remember you," Lorelei said.

"When you were little, your mom would bring you and Thomas over to play."

Lorelei leaned back in the chair and stared at Dee, trying to place her face. "You and your husband owned a little store in Charleston," Lorelei said, starting to remember.

"We did, and I've known your mom most her life. We lost touch when Harry, my late husband, and I sold our little store and moved. How is your mom doing?"

"She's out traveling," Lorelei said, "with her best friend."

"And your dad?"

"He passed away a few years ago."

"I'm so sorry," Dee said. "You've grown into a beautiful young lady. Where is Thomas now?"

"He's in Seattle, with his wife, Jessica. They have a financial advising business. They are doing pretty well"

They sat in silence again, listening to the sounds of the hospital as machines beeped, soft shoes padding on the floor outside in the hallway, the silent sobs of a family member in a next room to them, and down the hallway a drunk begging for a Subway sandwich.

The doctor opened the curtain again, leaving it open as he walked to the side of Dee's bed.

"Your X-rays show no damage. Your test results came back fine. You are in remarkable shape for a woman of sixty-five."

"And other than some bumps, bruises and scrapes from sliding down that bluff, I feel great," Dee said.

Lorelei looked at Dee. She had a healthy glow to her, looking younger than when Lorelei found her on the beach a few hours ago. Her long hair was out of her face, and she had been given a washrag to clean up. Lorelei was surprised. She thought Dee was an old woman.

"I'll be staying with her for the next few days, so if she needs to see her doctor I will be happy to take her to any appointments."

"Then I'll go get the release forms together." He left the room for the last time and didn't bother closing the curtain for them.

"Do you have clothes to wear home?" Lorelei asked, realizing that Dee was in a hospital gown.

"I'll just put my clothes back on. It won't be the first time I've had to put dirty clothes back on."

"That can be a story for a later time," Lorelei laughed as she turned to find Dee's clothes.

"They are in a plastic bag on the counter."

Lorelei noticed the bag sitting on the counter for the first time. "Do you need any help?" she asked.

"Only need you to hand me the bag. I can get dressed. I truly am fine. I'm just sore. Tomorrow will be a different story though. Do you have plans tomorrow or can you hang out with your old and yet new found friend?" Dee asked.

"I have as much time as you need. My only request is that Bindi can come over and play with your Lily. I don't want to leave her home alone. I feel bad leaving her as long as I have." Lorelei handed Dee the bag, and not waiting for a reply, she stepped out of the room and closed the curtain to allow Dee privacy while she got dressed. The curtain opened back up and Lorelei went back in as Dee settled herself on the edge of the bed, waiting to be released.

A nurse came into the room with some papers for Dee to sign. "I also have a prescription for you for pain. You may not think you need it now, but you will be feeling your fall tomorrow. And make an appointment with your primary caregiver to see him or her and get looked at."

Dee signed the papers and took the prescription from the

nurse, which Lorelei then took, then folded up before putting them in her pocket.

"I will get this filled for her tomorrow," Lorelei promised the nurse.

"You just get yourself healed and stay away from the bluffs," he said before leaving.

Once she was released, Lorelei helped escort Dee out of the hospital. She had Dee wait inside the emergency room lobby while she went and got her car. When she pulled up to the double doors, Dee got in and carefully put on her seatbelt before Lorelei pulled out of the parking lot.

They drove in silence for a couple miles before Lorelei asked, "Want to tell me what really happened? What aren't you telling the police?"

Tension filled the air and Lorelei decided to wait out Dee.

After another mile, Dee said, "I surprised a burglar, I think."

Lorelei did not say anything. She did not want to drag it out of this woman, she wanted Dee to trust her and tell her when she was ready.

"Were you attacked?" Lorelei finally asked.

"No, just startled. I ran to the trail and that's when I slipped."

They drove the rest of the way to Charleston without speaking. Lorelei had questions, but thought it best to get Dee settled before pushing her any further.

"Do you want me to stay with you tonight?" Lorelei asked before they got to the Charleston Bridge.

"Yes, if you don't mind," Dee said.

"Do you want me to take you home before I go to the Inn and get Bindi and some clothes?"

"I don't mind waiting in the car, or I can come in with you," Dee replied.

"If you don't mind walking up stairs you are more than

welcome to come inside."

"I can do stairs. I have stairs at my house I'll have to climb."

"I just don't want you to overdo it tonight," Lorelei replied as she pulled into her parking spot.

"I am not hurting, but I can't promise the same thing tomorrow. I'd rather not be alone. So I'll go with you." Dee undid her seatbelt and got out of the car before Lorelei.

"I'm upstairs, in unit 4, but the stairs aren't too bad. They are split in two rises, with shallow steps."

Lorelei unlocked the door to the lobby and held it opened for Dee. She waited for Dee to start up the stairs and followed behind.

"I'm at the top and to the left."

Dee took her time with each step. She moved slowly, holding the handrail as she made her way up. She turned left and waited for Lorelei to unlock the door. Once they were inside, Bindi jumped up onto the arm of the sofa and waited for someone to pet her; it turned out to be Dee. She started rubbing Bindi's ears and then scratched her under her chin.

"I cannot thank you enough," she leaned over and kissed Bindi on the nose, "for staying with me while your mom went and got help." Bindi looked over at her person before giving Dee kisses.

Lorelei went into the bedroom and packed enough clothes for a few days. She didn't know how long Dee would need her.

"Are you looking for a place to rent?" Dee called from the living room. She was sitting on the couch with Bindi in her lap.

"I am, but haven't started looking yet." Lorelei said as she stuffed her clothes into a small suitcase and then thought of the small apartment above Dee's garage.

"What are you looking for?"

"Something that when I walk into it, I am comfortable, and can stay there for as long as I need to while my place is being remodeled." She appeared back in the living room and set her bag on the kitchenette table.

"Oh, so you're staying in the area?" Dee asked.

"My grandparents had a house across the street from you. It needs some work done before I can move in. They left it to me so I guess I'm staying forever." Lorelei went into the bathroom and grabbed a few of her toiletries and put them in a smaller bag. She came out and sat in a chair next to the sofa.

"I may have the perfect place for you," Dee said as Bindi jumped off the couch and into Lorelei's lap. Her smile lit up her eyes.

"Do you want to tell me what you were keeping from the authorities?" Lorelei changed the subject as she pet Bindi.

"Can I trust you?" Dee asked.

"It's kind of a silly question to ask now that I have you in my home," Lorelei laughed.

"I guess you're right," she smiled, "and I will tell you, but first, do you have anything to drink in this place?"

"What did they give you at the hospital for pain? I don't want to give you something that will be against doctor's orders."

"I wouldn't let them give me anything stronger than Tylenol. I don't like prescription medications. I hate how they make me feel. And I am not getting that prescription filled so don't worry about that either."

Lorelei got up and went to the kitchenette and opened a cupboard. "I have a bottle of whiskey, which I do not care for, but it was a gift from a friend, or I have a bottle of Cabernet."

"A glass of Cabernet would be lovely, if you will have one with me," Dee replied.

"If I'm going to have a glass with you, why don't we take it to your house and then we can talk. I don't want to start drinking before taking you home. I am guessing this story will be longer than just one glass of wine."

"You are correct," Dee said, "and I have better stuff at my house."

"Then let's go." Lorelei found Bindi's harness and leash. Bindi bounced until Lorelei could catch her and get the harness on.

"She's quite the companion," Dee said as she watched the little dog wait patiently.

"She truly is. I got her as a rescue when she was about five months old. The family that got her was not ready for a dog smarter than themselves. This little dog has a mind of her own and will use it. She is so full of spunk that if we don't go for a run daily she lets me know by getting into anything she can find. Don't you, Bin?" Lorelei kissed Bindi's nose.

"She was lucky to have found you," Dee said.

"I think we were both lucky to have found each other."

Bindi waited just long enough for her person to put on her harness and attach the leash before starting bouncing again. Once Lorelei stood up, Bindi grabbed the leash in her mouth and started tugging her toward the door.

"Just a minute," Lorelei said as she pulled Bindi back so she could grab her overnight bag. "Let's go!" Bindi started jumping, never letting her leash out of her mouth.

"She is full of energy," Dee laughed as she stood up to leave.

"That's why I nicknamed her Bouncing Bindi," Lorelei said. "I hope she won't be too much for you, at your place."

"Are you kidding? That much energy will make the house feel young again. Poor Lily, she needs the exercise and companionship this little gal will surely be giving her."

They made their way back down to the car. Once they were seat belted in, with Bindi in the back seat, her feet on the armrest next to Lorelei, and her head between the front seats,

Lorelei pulled out and headed out toward the beaches, toward Dee's home, toward Lorelei's new home.

4

After making sure Dee was comfortable, sitting at the kitchen table, Lorelei looked through the cupboards for glasses. Bindi raced around the upstairs trying to get Lily, the golden retriever, to play with her. The sun had set, leaving the landscape dark. Lorelei could not see the view that Dee enjoyed daily. She found small glasses and brought them to the table.

"What would you like to drink?" Lorelei asked.

"I have some rum in the cupboard above the refrigerator. It's from a local distillery, about two miles from here."

"There's a local distillery?" Lorelei asked.

"Yes, been here for about five years, and they make some of the best rum, even if you aren't a rum drinker."

Lorelei opened the cupboard and saw a bottle of The Devil's Own Spiced rum. She poured them each a half ounce and joined Dee at the table.

"I wish there was still daylight so I could see your view," Lorelei said.

"You'll see it in the morning when we have coffee, as long as the clouds don't obscure it," Dee said.

"Your place sits higher than my grandparents' home, I

guess my home now, so I will get this view too," Lorelei said as she took the chair across from Dee.

Both women took a small taste of the rum. It was the best rum Lorelei ever had.

They sat, nursing their drinks, while watching Bindi still trying to get Lily to play. Lily tried to keep up with Bindi but ended up just sitting and watching Bind run circles around her with one Lily's stuffed toys in her mouth.

"Let me refill our drinks," Dee said as she stood. Lorelei was surprised to see her glass empty. She drank all her rum.

"No, you sit there and I will refill our glasses." Lorelei stood as Dee sat back down. She got the bottle and brought it back to the table. She refilled both glasses with about a half ounce again before putting the stopper the bottle. They sat for a few moments before Lorelei asked, "Are you ready to tell me what happened today?"

"Someone was in the house. It was a cop, or at least I think it was a cop. I saw a face and a uniform. I know it was a uniform because of the patches sown on it." Dee set her glass down and picked up a napkin. "I went over to feed the cat, and check the house. There was movement in the window and I saw a man and he was in a uniform, I know it was a uniform." A single tear slid down Dee's cheek. She wiped it away with the napkin. "I know about the old trail along the bluff because I've walked it many times with my friend, Fran. As I was trying to get to the neighbor's house, I tripped over my own feet and fell flat, then rolled. I slid part way down the bluff, but caught myself on an exposed root. I held on, and I tried to be quiet, but when I looked up, the man was standing above me. I lost my grip on the root and slid the rest of the way.

"I then I just laid there, in the sand, as still as I could be. What if he looked over the edge and saw me moving? He would come down and finish me off! I think maybe he thought the fall did me in. You showed up, it must have been a half hour later, but I don't know. And then you wanted to leave me! I know it was to get help, but I panicked. I am so grateful you left your Bindi with me." At the mention of her name, Bindi stopped trying to get Lily to chase her. "With Bindi, I didn't feel as vulnerable."

"Did the man know you saw him?" Lorelei asked.

"We locked eyes before I lost my grip, and he gave me this wicked smile that raised the hair on the back of my neck. All I know is I saw a man in uniform, so I'm not talking to any cops. He knows I saw him! What if he comes after me to shut me up?"

"But if it wasn't the officers who came down to the beach, why not talk to them?"

"How do I know they aren't in it together?"

Lorelei thought for a moment before answering, "I can understand why you didn't want to say anything in front of the police. But why were you wary of the EMT's?"

"Because they also wear uniforms."

Lorelei stared into her glass, thought for another moment before replying. "You're right, I would never have thought of a first responder as someone to worry about."

"When you came back with help with someone in a dark uniform I didn't know what to think," Dee whispered, "and the cops in the area wear the same dark uniforms, so I didn't know who to trust. But I was sure I could trust you."

"Why did you think you could trust me?" Lorelei asked.

"At first, I thought I recognized you, but mostly because you left your most precious possession with me; your dog. People don't leave their pets with strangers, unless they know there is no danger to their companion."

"How could I leave you alone while I went for help?" Lorelei asked.

"And that is how I knew I could trust you," Dee said as she

reached out and placed her hand on Lorelei's. Lorelei covered it with her own.

"Now what do we do?" Lorelei asked.

"First, if you are still looking for a place to live, I think my apartment above the garage would fit you perfectly. And the backyard is fenced so your Bindi would have a place to run and play while you are at work. And Lily would have someone to play with."

"I don't work," Lorelei admitted.

"What do you do for a living?" Dee asked.

"To be honest, nothing. I haven't found what I want to be when a grow-up." She upended her glass and finished off the last of the rum.

"What have you been doing since you left high school?"

"I have my Master's degree but would need a Doctorate to be considered for employment in my field of study."

"What did you study?" Dee asked as she added another half inch of rum to their glasses. The rum was going to Lorelei's head, but she wasn't driving so she figured one more drink wouldn't hurt, but it would have to be her last one.

"My degree is in Literature, but dabbled in Art, and had fun with writing. So I don't have anything that would help me land a job."

"So what are you going to do?" Dee asked.

"I am going to find out who was in that house, and why. You feel up to an adventure tomorrow?" A hiccup escaped Lorelei. She felt her cheeks flush as she tried to hide a giggle with the back of her hand.

"I am. Well, right now anyway." Dee said enthusiastically. She let out a sigh, "I don't know how I will feel in the morning. I do have to check on their cat since I wasn't able to today. You still didn't say what you do for money."

"Oh, that's an easy one, after making plans after college,

Mom won the lottery."

"How much are you worth?" Dee asked in disbelief.

"I'm not worth anything. Mom won close to $4 million, after taxes. She deposits money into our accounts each month so Thomas and I don't have to worry about whether we can pay our bills. Thomas and his wife both work, so I think they are putting the money away. But me, I'm taking advantage of it, and went to different places up and down the western coast. With my grandparents leaving me the house, it all worked out. This is where I chose to be."

"What house?" Dee asked.

"The small one across the street and one driveway down, toward the cove."

"Your mom's parents? I didn't know that," Dee exclaimed.

"No, those were Dad's parents. We would come down during the summer to visit them after we moved away. Mom's parents retired in Florida."

"I lost touch with so many people when we sold that little store. Harry and I enjoyed our early retirement and became home bodies."

"I know how that goes," Lorelei said, "I'd rather be a home body than have to deal with lots of people every day."

"And your mom, what is she doing now?"

"She's out traveling, having the time of her life. Dad died a few years ago. He was sick for years and prepared Mom for being without him. He made her promise to keep living. After he died, Mom's way of living was playing the lottery every week. She told herself if she ever won, she would take the trip of a lifetime."

"Did she expect to win?" Dee asked.

"No clue, Thomas and I thought she was delusional." Lorelei took another sip before continuing, "Guess it paid off. She and her best friend are on a cruise to Europe. She rented her house out, packed up, and left. Her best friend is also a widow so they are just enjoying themselves. She calls as often as she can, when she is near civilization or when her cell phone works, to share her adventure, and to see how Thomas and I are doing." Lorelei swirled her rum. She was always close with her mom, and being away at college, Lorelei stayed in constant contact. Now, she only hears from her mom every other week or so."With the money she gives us, we can't complain, though."

"And Thomas, how is he doing?"

"He's is married to a wonderful woman, Jessica, and they are having their first kid in about four months."

"Well, I'm glad you made your way here. Now, I need to get you set up with someplace to sleep." She stood and went to the office that was just off from the kitchen, opened a closet and pulled out some blankets and a pillow.

"What about your little apartment you were going to show me?" Lorelei asked.

"I don't think I can do anymore stairs tonight," Dee said, rubbing absently at her knees as she sat back down. "Plus, I would feel better having you in the house with me, just for tonight."

"I can do that."

"If you go into the kitchen, hanging inside the pantry door, you will find a set of keys," Dee said.

Lorelei went to the kitchen, found the set of keys, and handed them to Dee.

"This one is for the door, and this one is for the deadbolt," Dee said, holding up the keys. There were others on the ring, but Dee only mentioned the two Lorelei would need.

Lorelei hesitated for just a second before wrapping her arms around Dee, giving her a sincere hug. "I'll be here all night. And in the morning, I'll make the coffee and whatever you want for breakfast."

Dee hugged her back as she said, "I'm early riser so I may

have breakfast ready for you instead."

"Is it okay if I go look at the apartment right now? I can also check around outside and make sure not one is hanging around in the shadows."

"Of course you can," Dee said, "just remember to lock up when you come back inside."

Lorelei hooked the leash to Bindi's harness and grabbed her overnight bag before leaving the main house.

Once Bindi did her business Lorelei went up the steps to the apartment above the large garage. She didn't know what to expect, but upon entering, saw it was beautiful. It had all the comforts of home. It was decorated with art from the coast. Silk flowers sat in a vase on the dining room table. A tall avocado plant loomed in the corner. The only reason Lorelei knew what it was was because she always tried growing them from seeds every time she ate an avocado when she was in grade school. The large living area had a couch and two recliners, a large kitchen that could create any meal, and on one wall there was a door and a short hallway. The door led to a bedroom with a queen size bed, dresser, and closet. The hallway led to a bathroom with a full bath. The openness of the apartment was beyond what Lorelei was expecting. The windows faced West, giving her a full view of the ocean, that would be visible when the sun was up. Dee was right when she said she had the perfect place for Lorelei. And she would be right across the street from her own little home while it was being remodeled.

5

The rising sun brought in the morning light, waking Lorelei with a start. She had forgotten where she was for a moment as she sat up. Bindi was curled next to her, who stretched, yawned, then went back to sleep.

"Come on, we have work to do," she told Bindi as she slid her feet out from under the covers and dangled them over the edge of the couch.

Lorelei got up, realized she took all her stuff to the apartment last night, and decided she needed to get changed and brush her teeth before she did anything else. She grabbed the apartment keys, Bindi staying close to her heals as she left the main house and went back to the small apartment.

She went to the bathroom, then came back into the living area with her toothbrush in her mouth. She brushed her teeth as she looked out at the Pacific Ocean. Sure, there were houses on the other side of the road so she couldn't see the bluffs, but she could feel the pounding of the waves through the floor and could hear the roar. She went back into the bathroom to spit out her toothpaste.

"We need to get a tide book," she told Bindi as she came back from the bathroom. She went to find her overnight bag.

She pulled out a pair of purple sweats with a UW on one leg, and Go Dawgs on the other. Her t-shirt was from UW also.

It had been hard on Thomas that Lorelei hadn't gone to the same college as him. She had told him she needed to find out who she was. She couldn't spend her life known as Thomas's twin sister: You know the one, she got all the looks while Thomas got all the brains. It wasn't that Lorelei wasn't smart, but not many could get past her looks. Thomas could have been a rocket scientist if he wanted. There was nothing her brother couldn't do when he set his mind to it. Jessica, his wife, was the same way.

After going through the cupboards, Lorelei remembered she wasn't living here yet, and there would be no coffee for her no matter how hard she looked. Just as there would be no dog food for Bindi since she forgot to pack it last night.

As she opened the door to the apartment, she hadn't bothered with Bindi's leash since the back yard was fenced. She was just going down the stairs and across the sidewalk. Lily was already outside and Bindi rushed down the steps to her before Lorelei closed the apartment door.

"Come on in," Dee said as Lorelei neared the open door. "Coffee is fresh and I have bagels with cream cheese sitting on the table."

"Wow, thanks!" Lorelei said as she walked in. "I hope I didn't wake you when we left this morning."

"Of course not, I told you I was an early riser," Dee said.

"Do you have cream for the coffee too?"

"Who drinks coffee without cream? No one, that's who," Dee said as she slowly led Lorelei up the stairs.

"You seem to be moving okay today," Lorelei said as she waited for Dee to reach the top of the landing, before joining her there.

"I've been taking my Ibuprofen and Tylenol and it's been helping. I felt like an old woman when I tried to get out of bed this morning, so I soaked in a nice hot bath until I felt my normal self. That's where I was when you thought you snuck out."

"I must admit, you look more my mom's age than my grandmother's age this morning," Lorelei said as she found cups, along with the coffee urn on the table with the bagels. She poured herself a large cup of coffee, added cream from the small pitcher, then took a long drink. The coffee was a dark roast, with wonderful flavors that filled her senses. Just as she sat down Bindi came charging up the steps with Lily right behind, did a few circles around the kitchen, then ran in between the living room furniture, before heading back down the stairs and outside.

"Lily will be getting more exercise today than she has in four years," Dee said as she saw the look of concern on Lorelei's face. Dee poured herself a cup of coffee, added a fair amount of cream and two teaspoons of sugar before sitting at the table with Lorelei.

"I am so sorry!" Lorelei sputtered, "Bindi is such a spitfire and full of energy, which is why I run with her every morning. I did not mean to leave the door open and have her tear around your house."

Dee reached out and patted Lorelei's hand, "This house needs excitement. I can't think of a better way to achieve that than to have a little dog give my Lily a good morning workout. Honestly! Plus, I couldn't wait for you two to get here this morning! My life has been so boring, I am ready to shake things up."

"Wait, what?" Lorelei's hand was almost to her mouth for her first bite of a cream cheese covered bagel, a food she allows herself rarely.

"We need to find who that man was in Jim and Fran's house yesterday. And I still need to feed their cat!" Dee said as she wiggled in her seat, antsy to go but Lorelei just stared.

"I think finding out who was in that house is a priority!"

"We can't go without a plan. The two of us can check out the house together, but after that, I will see what I can find out alone. And what a better way than by someone who is new to the area, who people don't know."

"I can drive, and and you can ask the questions."

Lorelei shook her head. "This is something I should do alone. I can ask my questions, pretending I am learning about the area while really try to figure out what's going on."

"I guess I can see your point," Dee set her coffee down and grabbed her bagel. She didn't take a bite. Instead she huffed, "When that cop, or whoever that man was in Jim and Fran's house, saw me, who's to say he didn't recognize you when you found me?" The excitement was dimming a bit from Dee's eyes but she was still ready to go.

"My hair was up and I was in big baggy sweats. I was at the bottom of the bluff. I don't think the man was there when I found you, and I am pretty sure if he looked over and saw you lying in the sand, he was not going to stick around and wait for you to be found."

"I'm just glad he didn't come down there to finish me off!" Dee drained her coffee cup and poured another half a cup.

"I was thinking about this last night, and what we should do," Lorelei said, in between bites of bagel, "is go to the house this morning, feed the cat, and then look around to see if anything is missing. And depending on what we find, we may need to call the police."

"We can't call the police!" Dee exclaimed, setting her cup down hard, spilling some of the coffee. She turned to look out the big bay window. Lorelei watched Dee's eyebrows furrowed. "I could get in trouble for making a false police report last night, and because I think it was a cop."

"You didn't make a police report, I was there, you kept saying nothing happened, so you're fine. I understand you being wary about going to the police, but they need to be informed, depending on what we find."

"And if I start saying I saw a cop there? Someone in uniform?" Dee asked.

"You still didn't make a formal report, so you did nothing wrong by not saying something earlier. And I think they would understand. And if we find something, I will look into it so you still don't have to call the cops until we need to." Lorelei popped the last bite of bagel into her mouth, licked her fingers clean, then finished her coffee. She really wanted a second cup, but that would have to wait. She stood, turned and stopped as she took in Dee's view of the ocean. A few trees were in the way, and the roof tops of houses kept her from seeing the bluffs. What she did see, as she looked out, were the large rock formations and the waves breaking on them, shooting spray up in the air. Lorelei watched, as wave after wave crashed on the rocks. She could feel the pounding surf, in her feet, and in her chest, as the sounds made their way to her soul.

"Why would anyone want to live anywhere else?" she whispered, almost to herself.

"So, I guess this means you'd like to move into that apartment I have," Dee said.

"I'll be moving in today, which will take about an hour since all I have is a suitcase and Bindi's stuff." Lorelei suddenly remembered, "I don't have any food for Bindi, I forgot to bring it last night. Can she share some of Lily's food until I get her's?"

"Of course," Dee said. She went to the kitchen and fetched a dog bowl from a pantry that Lorelei hadn't noticed, and filled it with dog food.

"She doesn't eat that much!"

"Half is for Lily, and as they eat, we can go across the street to Jim and Fran's house."

With the dogs fed, Lorelei and Dee made their way down the stairs and out into Dee's driveway. As they walked, Dee paced slowed until she was stopped half way to Jim and Fran's driveway.

"If you see anyone that puts you on edge, just elbow me hard, that way we don't have to say anything to cause suspicion," Lorelei said as she watched Dee's eyes widen.

"What if I accidentally elbow you, if I slip or fall or something?" Dee asked, tentatively taking another step forward.

"Don't make this more complicated than it needs to be. Maybe just reach over and grab my hand."

"So which is it?" Dee asked, as she slowly started walking again. "Do I grab your hand or elbow you?"

"Just grab my hand," Lorelei said.

"What if I can't reach you? Then what do I do?"

"You stay calm and make your way to me." Lorelei slipped her arm into Dee's as Dee turned into the driveway of a large home that faced the ocean. "I am not going to be very far from you, I'm guessing within reach at all times because I'm worried about you."

"Why are you worried about me?" Dee asked as Lorelei made her way toward the back door.

"Because you had a scare," Lorelei said, as Dee headed the other direction, toward the front of the house, facing the ocean.

Dee's nerves were getting the better of her as she started rambling, "I've been feeding Mr. Kitty for the last week or so. They usually go on vacation for about two weeks every other month. They are both retired and love to spend time in Paris. Their eldest granddaughter lives there with her husband and now with their first great grand baby, which is why they are gone for a month this time. And to be honest, I am waiting for them to just move there."

Lorelei didn't notice the rambling, she was stuck on the name of the cat. "Who names their cat Mr. Kitty? I mean, I've known people to name their cat's Kitty, or Miss Kitty, or some variation, but a male cat?"

"A granddaughter," Dee hesitated, looked up for a moment, like she was waiting for the answer to float down on the cool ocean breeze, "when she was six or eight?"

"You know, Jim's retired Coast Guard, and she's a lawyer. That is how we met."

"You're a lawyer?" Lorelei asked.

"No, my husband and I retained her while we had the little shop in Charleston. We had this yard toy, a giraffe mounted on a large spring about this big around." She made the motion of hugging a tree where her hands met on the opposite side. "The giraffe was made of some sort of caste iron, I think. We had it in the yard for kids to play on while their parent's shopped."

"I don't remember that when we would come visit," Lorelei said. She remembered two large blocks in the yard, that she and Thomas use to climb, but there was no giraffe.

"We had that giraffe well before your time, but some little kid bumped his nose on it and the parents tried to sue us, Harry and me. We hired Fran, who had a small practice next to us. We didn't get sued, but we did have to remove the giraffe. The kids had nothing to do while the parents shopped. So we brought in those big blocks of wood. They were huge, and the kids would play on those. And no one got hurt."

"I remember those, Thomas and I played on them."

"There wasn't anyway for someone to get hurt so we were okay."

"What do you do now?" Lorelei asked. "This town is so small I am going to have to find something to do."

"I volunteer here and there," Dee said.

They walked up a few steps to the deck, and Lorelei couldn't see anything out of place. Dee pulled a set of keys out of her jacket pocket and unlocked the sliding glass door. They walked in and Lorelei noticed the house was furnished in an eclectic style. Furniture didn't match, but was put together room by room. She was sure they didn't go to yard sales, but maybe estate sales. The kitchen and dining room were done in oak, with a large table and a china cabinet. The cabinets were painted. Looking through to the living room, it had the style of an old victorian.

"This is quite a home," she said as she walked through.

"They like it this way. It was furnished when they bought it and they decided to leave it. Their personal touch is in the art." Dee said as she filled the cat's dish with food. Then she rinsed out the water bowl and poured in fresh water.

Lorelei was looking around the living room when Dee joined her. "Do you notice anything out of the ordinary?" she asked Dee.

"I'm not sure," Dee said as she walked around the room. She stopped by the sofa and looked around. "A painting is missing," she said as she looked at the wall above the large, stone fireplace.

"What kind of painting?" Lorelei asked.

"I'm not sure what the painting was, but I remember there was a large painting here."

Lorelei walked up and saw a nail in the bricks. She looked around and didn't see anything. "Is there anything else missing?" she asked.

Dee walked through the living room and into the bedroom. "I just can't be sure."

Lorelei went and stood next to her and saw another empty wall, where another painting could have hung.

"Was there something here?"

"I just don't remember," Dee said, letting out a heavy sigh.

"Do you know what the art was?"

"Paintings from their travels. They always brought home something from the places they visited."

They walked through the large home and looked to see if anything else was missing. Dee couldn't be sure.

"Someone came in and took their large painting." Dee said as she went back into the kitchen. The food bowl sat untouched.

"Where's the cat?" Lorelei asked.

"I don't know, he's an indoor cat so he should be here somewhere." Dee started calling the cat, but he didn't come out from wherever he was hiding.

"I'll look outside," Lorelei said and went back outside.

She made her way back outside and walked around the house and saw something on the ground. She bent and picked up a matchbook. She continued to the spot where she assumed Dee had slipped. She noticed many shoe prints on the trail. She made her way back inside and showed the matchbook to Dee.

"Do you recognize this?" She handed it to Dee who turned it over in her hands.

"This is from one the casinos that's in town, The Mill Casino. I wonder if the person who was here dropped it. Jim and Fran don't smoke, or allow smoking in their house. Maybe we should go there," Dee said, "and see if the man I saw is there. They have security guards, maybe that was who was here."

"You can't go there," Lorelei said as she took the matchbook back. "Remember, he may recognize you and you could be putting yourself in danger. I can go, take pictures of the security guards. Then you can let me know if you recognize any of them."

"I couldn't ask you to do that!"

"You aren't asking, I'm volunteering. I'll just take photos

with my phone. We can look at them when I get back."

"I don't think you can do that," Dee said.

"Why? What are they going to do if I'm taking pictures?"

"They'll kick you out, and what if that security guard sees you taking pictures? You could be putting yourself in danger, as well," Dee huffed.

"Nonsense, I'll be sneaky and no one will know. I'll get pictures and come back and we can go through them. And I will be with so many people he won't risk exposing himself."

Dee chewed her bottom lip.

"I will be okay, honest."

"Okay," Dee finally agreed, "but first we need to find their cat, I can't leave without knowing he's okay."

"We will find him," Lorelei said as she started walking through the house again, calling the cat. Dee followed her, calling out too.

After a few minutes, Lorelei said, "I'll go back outside and call him. Maybe he escaped when the door was open." She went back out the kitchen door and started calling.

"Mr. Kitty, where are you?" She walked around the house and kept calling. After a few minutes she heard a quiet mewing.

"Mr. Kitty, come out, Mr. Kitty." Lorelei felt silly calling a cat by that name but kept calling. The mewing got louder as she walked to the front of the house. She looked around and saw a large black cat on the garage roof. "Mr. Kitty, come on down."

Dee came outside and was calling the cat.

"I think he's here," Lorelei called out to her. Dee came around the corner and looked in the direction of the noise.

"Mr. Kitty, how did you get up there?" Dee said as she found the source of the noise.

"Is there an upstairs? Or maybe a ladder so we can get him down?" Lorelei asked.

"There's a ladder in the garage, the house has an attic but no windows to open to get to him."

Lorelei went to the garage at the back of the house. She pulled on the door but it wouldn't open. She tugged one more time before giving up. She went back to where Dee stood, calling the cat. "I can't open the garage door, I think I need to go back into the house and get in that way. I'll get the ladder and meet you here."

Back inside, Lorelei looked around until she found a door that led in the direction of the garage. Once inside she found a ladder and then went to the door and looked for a way to open it. There was a keypad but she didn't know the combination. She grabbed the ladder and dragged it through the house and out the door. She carried it to where she had left Dee, who was still talking to the cat. She leaned it against the wall and started climbing up to the garage roof.

"Mr. Kitty," she called as she got level with the roof. The black cat mewed at her before coming toward her. When he was close, Lorelei reached out and grabbed him. He yowled at her as she pulled him toward her. Lorelei tucked him under her arm as he protested before she started back down the ladder. Once she got to the last rung, Dee took the cat from her and carried him inside the house. Lorelei followed her, dragging the ladder once again. Mr. Kitty went straight to his food and started eating.

"He didn't eat yesterday," Dee said as she watched him.

"It's not your fault," Lorelei said as she put her hand on Dee's shoulder. "He's home and safe. Let's go back to your house and figure out what we're going to do next."

As they left the house, Dee double checked to make sure the door was locked.

6

Back at Dee's house, Bindi and Lily bounded out of the house as soon as Dee opened the door. Bindi ran off in search for a toy, with Lily trailing after her. The two women made their way upstairs to the living room.

"What's your plan?" Dee asked.

"I think I'll head to the casino tonight and take pictures. We can regroup in the morning and go through the photos."

"Sounds like a solid plan," Dee said. "Would you like something to eat? I was planning on making some pasta for dinner."

"That would be great, would you like me to run to the store for anything before I head out tonight?"

"If you don't mind, I would love some french bread. Do you like mushrooms?"

"Chicken, mushrooms and broccoli," Lorelei said.

"I'll give you a list," Dee said as she made her way to her desk. She found her note pad and wrote out what she needed. She handed it to Lorelei who looked it over.

"Can I leave Bindi here while I get this?"

"Of course you can. Lily will be happy to play with her while you're gone."

"Then I will be back soon," Lorelei said as she headed for the door. "I wouldn't let Bindi out, otherwise she will bark until I get home. It's why I never leave her outside."

"She doesn't bark inside?"

"No, she knows she needs to behave inside. We use to live in an apartment and our neighbors were petty. Complained about everything, even if I walked across the floor before their alarm went off. So, I worked with her like the devil, to teach her she had an inside voice while I was gone. It took about a month and so may complaints, but we persevered. I think the manager liked Bindi and me better than the tenants who constantly complained."

"Then have no worries!"

Lorelei ripped a small piece of paper from the list Dee handed her and wrote her cell number on it, handed it to Dee, "In case you need to get a hold of me." She looked at the grocery list as she headed for the stairs that would lead her outside. "Bindi, you need to be a good girl, and I'll be back."

Bindi's person scratched her ears and rubbed under her chin before leaving her in this new place. Bindi ran to the window so she could watch her person leave. She knew not to bark, her person would be back. Lorelei climbed into her Honda. The car was old but started on the first attempt.

She made her way into town and went to Safeway. She pulled out the list before entering the store, looking to see what Dee needed for dinner. She went in and picked up the few things that were needed for the pasta, dog food, coffee and creamer. One her way back home she went the long way so she could drive past the casino, wondering how best to implement her plan.

Lorelei thought on the way back home that she needed to go through the little apartment and make a list of what she would need to get through the next few months as her place was being remodeled. She hadn't brought anything with her when she moved to town. She was hoping to find a little furnished house to rent, but this new arrangement would work out better for her, being her home she inherited was right across the street.

Back at Dee's, she grabbed the groceries and carried them upstairs.

"I need to figure out what I'll need for the apartment," Lorelei said as she helped Dee with the food.

"The apartment is furnished, you only need to buy yourself some groceries. And whatever personal touches you want to add to it. My husband and I lived in it for a couple years while the house was being built. It just made more sense to keep it as it was and buy everything new for the house."

Lorelei looked up at the clock on the wall and saw it saw already after one. "Are you making dinner now?" she asked Dee.

"I like having it ready but I usually eat early anyway. It will be here for you when you're hungry."

"I need to go empty out the place I was renting and let them know I'll be moving out today. I'm also going to pick up groceries on my way back from the casino. I can't keep coming over here to eat. Though it is nice having company."

"You do what you need to do," Dee said as she set water on to boil.

"Bindi, let's go!"

Bindi bound down the steps and waited for her person at the door.

"Let's go check out our place," Lorelei said as she reached the door. She was carrying the bag that held the dog food, coffee, and creamer. As she opened the door, Bindi led her to their new place.

In the small apartment, she set the dog food and coffee on the counter and put the creamer in the refrigerator. Lorelei looked around, wondering what she should get to make this place her own. She had clothes, all of Bindi's belongings, and her toiletries. She couldn't think of anything else she would really need until she moved into her own home. She gathered Bindi and went to pack up what she had left behind

Back at the Charleston Inn, she started packing her suitcase with all her belongings. She emptied the closet and dresser, went into the bathroom and emptied it as well. Once she finished, she looked at what she had. Such a minimal existence, but that was okay. She didn't need much.

She called the manager and made arrangements to leave the key with the neighbor since she would not be coming back here. She loaded the little Honda and left, taking her stuff back to her new little apartment. After unloading the car, she set up Bindi's bed, toy box and food bowls. She filled the water bowl with fresh water and filled up the food bowl. Bindi ate when she needed to, and didn't over eat.

Lorelei took her suitcases to the bedroom and opened them on the bed. She pulled out a pair of Levi's and a sweatshirt. After changing, she pulled her long hair into a ponytail, and pulled it through the back of her baseball cap. She looked in the mirror. Pretty sure she was would be carded since she looked more like a twelve year old rather than her twenty-six years.

"I've got to go out now, you stay here and be a good girl." Lorelei picked up Bindi and gave her a hug. She placed her on the couch before locking up and leaving. She needed to remember to get a set of keys made and return the extra to Dee.

She left, wondering how she was going to get pictures inside the casino. She needed to figure out a way to take pictures of the security guards and not get caught. And she hoped Dee could identify one of them.

7

The Mill Casino's parking lot was full. Cars filled most of the parking lot and she noticed that the motor home parking was full as well. She looked up at the marquise and saw that it welcomed a Motor Home convention. It also welcomed people to a Jazz festival. The place would be packed. Hopefully she wouldn't be noticed taking pictures.

The first thing that struck her, as she walked in, was the cigarette smoke. The casinos were exempt from the indoor smoking ban. The air system kept the fresh air circulating, but if you weren't a smoker, the air smelled like a stale ashtray.

Lorelei pulled a twenty from her wallet and found a machine to play. She bet small so her money would last while she looked around the casino, trying to make up her mind on how best to take pictures and not be noticed. She kept hitting the minimum bet button as she scoped out the place. Bells started ringing around her. She looked to see who had won before realizing it was her machine. She hit a $4500 jackpot!

Great, Lorelei thought. She was doing what she could to be inconspicuous and now she was drawing attention to herself. Her machine stopped, the words "Wait for attendant" flashed across her screen. In a few minutes an attendant and security guard came to her side. She slipped out her phone and tried to get a picture of him, but had to put it away with all the people coming around.

"Congratulation, you hit the jackpot!" a spunky blonde said. "You need to follow me to cash in your winnings."

"Wait, I want to get a picture of this." Lorelei pulled out her phone and started taking pictures of the machine's screen, showing the jackpot. She then changed the direction of her camera and started taking pictures of those who were surrounding her. She was able to capture the image of the security guard. With the security guard following behind them, the attendant walked Lorelei to one of the cash windows.

"We have a winner!" the blonde said to the attendant. The security guard just stood there.

The attendant pulled out a form and filled it out. "You need to fill out your information and Milt here," she motioned to the big man still standing behind Lorelei, "can escort you to your car, if you need."

"I think I'll keep playing," Lorelei said. She took her cash and stuffed it in her sweatshirt's front pocket, but not before she handed the attendant a forty dollar tip and then gave the security guard another forty dollars. She hoped tipping was appropriate.

This was not going how she wanted it to. She wanted to stay under the radar and not be noticed. That was going to happen now.

She went back to the same machine and put in another twenty.

"I didn't picture you as a gambler," a deep voice said behind her.

She turned in her seat to see a tall man standing behind her. She recognized his face but couldn't place him.

"Am I that memorable?" he laughed.

"I'm sorry," Lorelei gave him her best smile that could light up a room, or so she was told.

"Michael Smith, one of cops that helped your friend," he said as he stuck out his hand.

"Oh," she said as she hesitated for a moment before grabbing his hand to shake it.

"Lorelei," she said, "Lorelei Silence."

"I remember," Michael stood there for a few awkward minutes.

"You look different out of your cop's uniform."

"I'm here visiting my parents. They are part of the motorhome convention. Since they retired, they travel all over the states for these conventions."

"Kind of like having a party everywhere they go?" she asked, stifling a laugh with the back of her hand.

"I guess you could say that. They are taking me to dinner here at one of the restaurant. I'm just waiting for them."

Lorelei stared into his blue eyes, wondering if she should continue talking with him. After all, she was here helping Dee, and not calling the police, to let them know what she learned.

Michael stared back. He wanted to spend some time with her, get to know her, but wasn't exactly sure how to make that happen.

"I'm not meeting them for another hour. Would you like to hang out for a bit, maybe see if some of your luck will help me at the Black Jack table?" Michael finally asked.

"I can do that," Lorelei replied, thinking this would give her a better opportunity to get more photos if she was with someone, instead of lurking around the machines on her own.

A smile spread across Michael's face, he was not expecting her to accept.

"So, you're a player," she said.

"No," he laughed. "The only time you'll catch me in the

casino is when the convention brings my parents to town. I see them every few months. And by that time I forget about my losses at the tables and am able to enjoy myself."

"I've never gambled before," Lorelei said.

"Don't let beginner's luck keep bringing you back," Michael said as he gently placed his hand at the small of her back, directing her to one of the Black Jack tables. He took a seat and placed a hundred on the table in exchange for some chips.

"Maybe my beginner's luck will bring you some good fortune tonight," she said as she took her place standing just behind his chair. She pulled her cell phone out and held it at her midsection. She looked down making sure she hit the camera button. She kept her finger in place to take pictures as she moved around. There were four other men at the table playing with Michael. She turned her body slightly, trying to take pictures of the dealer and the security who were walking around.

Michael won three hands in a row, tripling his money.

"I think you just may be good luck," he said as he pulled the last pile of chips to him.

"Maybe you can be my good luck charm," the elderly gentleman to Michael's right said. Lorelei noticed his pile of chips was quite small compared to Michael's pile.

"She's my good luck charm, and I don't share," Michael laughed as he placed another bet. Lorelei absentmindedly let her hand drift from the back of Michael's chair to his shoulder. He could feel the warmth of her through his shirt, and liked how it felt.

"Guess I'll have to find my own," the older gentleman laughed as he pulled more money from his wallet and exchanged the bills for more chips.

"I don't need lady luck," the burly man to Michael's left said. "I don't come in expecting to lose."

Lorelei kept her phone in front of her and kept taking pictures.

"What is that clicking noise?" Michael asked as he looked around.

"Oh, sorry, it's my text message alert. Let me put my phone on silent." She checked her phone as she turned it over. She was bumped by a couple who were making their way to one of the poker tables. She flicked the button to silence on her phone before she continued to snap pictures.

Michael won two more hands before he lost one.

"I need to use the lady's room," Lorelei leaned down to whisper in Michael's ear, "I'll be right back."

"Don't be gone too long, this is my best winning streak."

As Lorelei looked for the restroom, she took more pictures. She took the long way around, trying to get as many snapshots as she could, keeping her phone down out of sight.

"Ma'am, I have to ask you not to take pictures." A tall man in a dark suit said as he placed a hand on her shoulder.

"Pictures?" She tried to act surprised but what came out was guilt.

"Yes, we don't allow pictures in here." He kept his heavy hand on her shoulder.

"I'm sorry…" she trailed off, trying to think of what to say. "I just, my boss is sure a few of his employees are gambling and he asked me to take some pictures, I didn't know I wasn't able to."

"Just put your phone away. And don't let him send you to snoop on his employees. If he has any questions, he needs to come down himself."

"I'm sorry," Lorelei said as she shoved her phone into her sweatshirt pocket with all the cash.

"Thank you," he said, then turned to leave.

Lorelei made sure she was hidden from view in the restroom before pulling her phone back out. She then stuffed it back in her pocket and decided she would look at the pictures when she was back home. She found an empty stall, went to the bathroom, washed her hands, and then left. She made her way to a small bar and grabbed a beer on tap to help steady her nerves before making her way back to the Black Jack table. Michael still had a large pile of chips in front of him. The man to his right was gone and replace by another. The man to his left was still there and his pile of chips had grown. Lorelei couldn't tell how much he had but she was sure it was more than Michael. She ventured to pull out her phone and get a few more pictures. She held her beer, trying to hide the fact she was taking more pictures. She especially wanted one of Michael, to see if Dee would recognize him, so she went around the table and took a few photos from the dealer's view. She slipped her phone in her back pocket and went back to stand behind Michael, resting one hand on his shoulder again. She finished her beer and placed the empty glass on the tray held by a waitress who passed by.

After a few more hands Michael took his winnings and excused himself, thanking the other players for a good game. He tossed a chip to the dealer. The dealer blushed and thanked him.

"How much do you leave for a tip?" Lorelei asked as she tucked her hand in his arm, not waiting for an invitation.

"I try to leave ten percent of what I win," he said as he led her to the restaurant at the back of the building.

"How much did you win?"she asked. "Or is that bad manners?"

"It's not bad manners if you're the lady luck who helps the gambler win." He stopped at the door to the restaurant.

"Do they have good food here?"

"You haven't been here?" he asked.

"No," she said. "I told you this was my first time coming. I'm not much of a gambler. After my dad passed away, my mom spent her money playing the lottery."

"I'm sorry," Michael said.

"Why are you sorry? You don't know me, my mom or my brother, which is, by the way, the only family I have."

"I just figured she lost her hard earned money by the way you're talking." Michael said, wondering where his parents were.

"Actually, she won, but because she won doesn't make me a frequent visitor to the casinos."

"Then why are you here?" Michael stared into Lorelei's green eyes. She stared back, not wanting him to think of her as weak if she looked away.

"Actually, I am here as a courtesy to a friend." Lorelei wished his parents would arrive so they did not have to continue this conversation.

"And who would that be?" Michael asked, not looking away from her.

"My boss," Lorelei lied, thinking of the lie she told the security guard. "She suspects one of her employees of embezzling and wanted to know if she has a gambling problem."

"Does she?" he asked.

"I don't know. I haven't looked around enough to see."

"Where do you work? I thought you just moved here, a couple days ago," he said as his eyes narrowed slightly.

Lorelei's face reddened as he caught her in a lie. She looked around and found a handsome couple approaching them. The man had the same strong features as Michael, and the woman's blue eyes and blonde hair were the same as her son's.

Michael stepped back from Lorelei, "Mom, Dad, I'd like you to meet my friend, Lorelei. I ran into her in the casino."

"It's so nice to meet a friend of Micky's," his mom said. "We meet him often but he never brings a friend."

"Especially a friend as beautiful as you," Michael's father continued.

Lorelei felt her cheeks flush.

"That's unfair," Michael said. "You know I work too many hours to have a personal life."

"It's nice to finally meet one of Micky's friends." His mom held her hand out to Lorelei, which Lorelei reached out to shake.

"Welcome to the family," his dad said as he shook her hand.

"Why don't you join us for dinner," his mother asked, and without waiting for an answer turned to her husband and said, "That's alright with you, isn't it Mike?"

"Um… sure. If it's okay with Michael, I mean," Lorelei stammered as a blush crept across her face.

Michael held Lorelei's elbow and walked with her into the restaurant, as an answer to her question, and was followed by his parents.

"I have reservations for Smith. It was for three, but I need a table for four. I didn't realize my girlfriend had the evening off."

"Follow me," the hostess said. She grabbed the menus and another place setting before leading them to a bay front table.

"Really?" Lorelei laughed quietly, leaning toward Michael so only he could hear, "Your girlfriend?"

"I could have said I met you at the bar."

Lorelei gently punched Michael's arm.

"A man could do worse than having a woman like you on his arm," he said.

"Give me a break!" Lorelei pulled off her baseball cap and let her hair out of the ponytail bindings. Her red hair cascaded down her back in unruly curls.

"I guess you don't look in a mirror that often," Michael said as the reached the table. He pulled out her chair. Lorelei sat down and he took the seat next to her. His mom sat across from him and his dad sat across from Lorelei.

The hostess handed out the menus. Lorelei left hers sitting in front of her. Her thoughts wandered back to Dee. What was she doing here? She was here to help find the man who robbed the house Dee was taking care of, not have dinner with a cop and his parents.

"How long have you two been dating?" Michael's mom asked.

The heat from her embarrassment reached clear to Lorelei's ears as she felt them burned. She was grateful she let her hair down.

"Mom, I told you, she is just a friend," Michael said.

"And yet you told the hostess differently," Lorelei jested, as a way to make the situation more bearable. "Anyway, it's nice to meet you, um..." Lorelei didn't know how to address them.

"I'm so sorry," Michael interrupted, "these are my parents, Ann and Mike."

"It's nice to meet you, Ann and Mike," Lorelei said, relaxing a bit.

"Micky, what do you recommend?" Ann asked, after giving Lorelei a warm smile.

"Everything here is good, you really can't go wrong." Michael said as he picked up his menu.

Lorelei followed his example and picked up her own menu. Now she wanted a cheese burger but didn't want to order something so ordinary. She would just order something lite since she knew Dee had dinner waiting for her at the house.

"So," Lorelei smiled at Michael, "what do I call you? Michael or Micky?"

"Michael," he said as the color on his cheeks rose.

"Oh, you can call him Micky, most his family does," Ann

laughed.

The waitress showed up and put the uncomfortable conversation to a halt.

"What can I get y'all?" she asked. Lorelei hadn't heard anyone use that expression since she came to Oregon.

"Lorelei?" asked Michael.

"I'll have just have a dinner salad."

"And anything to drink," the waitress asked.

"I'd like a Corona with lime."

The waitress wrote it down before continuing around the table.

Ann Smith ordered the fresh grilled salmon with steamed vegetables. Mike ordered Prime Rib along with his son, who added a baked potato and whatever vegetables were served with it.

"Anything else for drinks?" the waitress asked.

"I'd like a Whiskey Sour," Ann Smith said.

Lorelei caught the look Michael and his dad exchanged. If she hadn't been looking at Michael, she would have missed it.

"I'd like a coffee," Mike said.

"And I'll have a Corona with lime, too," Michael said.

Lorelei couldn't help but wonder if she made a mistake asking for a beer.

After the waitress walked away to place their order, Michael leaned toward Lorelei and said, "You could have had more than a salad."

"Oh, I'm not afraid to eat, trust me, but I have dinner waiting for me at home."

"I guess this was spur of the moment for you," he said with good humor.

The dinner was good, the company was wonderful, except the glances between Michael and his father when Ann ordered a second, then a third Whiskey Sour. Lorelei didn't order another beer but asked for water when the waitress came back to check on them. She nursed the first beer, but had not finish it by the time dinner was done.

"I don't mean to cut the evening short, but I have an early appointment in the morning," Michael said after he finished his meal. "I'm on call so I have to be up before six."

"And I have some business to finish before I can call it a night," Lorelei said, following Michael's lead.

Ann Smith swirled the ice cubes in the empty glass. "I guess we should be going too."

"Will we see you before we have to leave?" Mike asked.

"When are you leaving town?" Michael asked as the waitress handed Mike the check.

"We are leaving Sunday morning," Ann said as she kept swirling the ice.

"How about I take you out to breakfast," Michael said. "There is a good restaurant across the street, and about a quarter mile north of the light."

"Will you bring your charming friend with you?" Ann slurred.

Lorelei's cheeks flushed as Michael looked at her.

"If she's not working," he said.

Lorelei didn't know if he was giving her a way out or if he was leaving it up to her to decide.

"Sunday? I'll check my calendar and get back to Michael," Lorelei said, not knowing if this was the correct answer.

"Then it's set!" Ann said, a big smile crossed her rosy face. "We will see you two Sunday morning! What is the name of the restaurant?"

"The Pancake Mill," Michael answered, looking between his father and Lorelei for acknowledgement.

"It's a date," Ann said as she stood. She held the table's edge to keep her balance.

"Let's get you up to our room," Mike put his arm around his wife and carefully helped her out of the restaurant.

"They aren't staying in their motorhome?" Lorelei asked after his parents left.

"It's too far for her to walk in her, um, condition."

"I'm sorry," Lorelei said, "if I had known, I would never had ordered a beer."

Michael watched until his parents were out of site, his shoulders slumped, his eyes were tired. "She would have ordered it whether you ordered a beer or not. She's been struggling with health issues and decided it was easier to deal with them with alcohol."

"I'm so sorry," Lorelei said again.

"It is what it is," Michael said as he led her out of the restaurant.

Lorelei couldn't help herself, she turned and wrapped her arms around Michael, hugging him close, trying to erase the sorrow she'd seen in his eyes. He held her for a moment before pulling away, the sad look still in his eyes, as he walked with her.

They meandered through the casino, her arm tucked neatly in his, until they were both at the entrance doors.

"Can I walk you to your car?" Michael asked.

"I have a bit more work to do," Lorelei said as she reached into her purse. She pulled out a pen and grabbed Michael's hand. "You can call me if you want to see me at breakfast Sunday." She wrote her number on Michael's hand. "I feel like I'm back in junior high," she laughed.

"You're the first girl to write her number on my hand," he said, smiling at her.

They stared at each other for a moment before Michael leaned over and kissed Lorelei on the cheek. "I'll give you a call tomorrow to see if you're free Sunday morning." He stared into her green eyes.

"And I will let you know that I will be there," she said. She squeezed his hand before turning to head back into the casino. She turned back to see him watching her walk away. She waved before heading into the crowd.

Lorelei sneaked a few more pictures before calling it a night.

She made it home close to nine o'clock. She didn't see any lights on at Dee's so she went straight home to the little apartment above the garage. She didn't get any groceries since her night was high jacked by Michael and his parents. She would go to town in the morning, after showing Dee the photos she was able to get.

Bindi was whining at the door as she slipped the key in the lock.

"Let's go outside," Lorelei said as she went back downstairs, following Bindi who took off into the dark side of the yard. Lorelei could hear the jingle of her collar even though she lost sight of her.

"Go potty, Bin," Lorelei called out after a few minutes. "It's bed time."

The door to Dee's house opened and Lily came bounding out and she chased after Bindi. Dee stood in the doorway.

"I didn't mean to disturb you," Lorelei said.

"Nonsense," Dee said. "Lily always goes out around nine. I'm just glad to see it's you here and not some dark figure lurking, waiting for me to be alone."

"I'm sorry I was out so late. I meant to be home sooner," Lorelei started before being cut off by Dee.

"It's fine. I may have had a scare but it's okay now," Dee told her.

"Tonight?" Lorelei's hand went to her mouth. Bindi bounded over and sat between her and Dee.

"No," Dee laughed, "from the fall. It's been quiet here."

"Okay, I got some pictures if you want to go through them."

"How about you come in, I have a plate of pasta waiting for you, but we can look at the photos in the morning over coffee," Dee said as she waited for Lily to come back.

"I lost track of time, and I would've called but din't have your number."

"I'll make sure you have it before you head out again," Dee said as they made their way to the kitchen. Dee pulled a plate out of the refrigerator and handed it to Lorelei. "You have a microwave at your place so you can heat it up. And I'll see you in the morning."

"What time?" Lorelei asked.

"Is seven too early for you?" Dee asked.

"I'll be there. Do you still have bagels and cream cheese?"

"Of course I do!"

Lorelei and Bindi went home to their little apartment and Lorelei ate the pasta, sharing it with Bindi.

8

The sound of rain pelting the windows woke Lorelei. Bindi was still curled up at the end of the bed on an old blanket of Lorelei's. Lorelei sat up and rubbed the sleep from her eyes before getting out of bed. Her feet scuffed along the carpet as she made her way to the bathroom. Before she had a chance to close the door, Bindi was in the bathroom with her.

"I can go by myself," she said as she nudged Bindi out of the bathroom with her foot before closing the door.

Bindi decided, after moving in with her person, that she needed to be with her every morning. It was a daily routine with them. Bindi tried to shove her nose under the door, sniffing to make sure her person was still in there, and hadn't left from a different exit, as she did every morning. Lorelei would reassure her, as she did every morning, that she hadn't snuck away, the whole time she was behind the closed door.

Lorelei used the restroom, washed her hands, brushed her hair and teeth, before deciding she was awake enough to get dressed in sweats and a t-shirt and go visit Dee. Back in the bedroom, she grabbed the Levi's she wore last night but tossed them in the corner, along with the sweatshirt she'd worn. The clothes smelled like cigarette smoke. Last thing she wanted to do was walk around smelling like an ashtray.

"Let's go, Bin," she called as she grabbed her cell phone. She checked the time. Just a little after seven so she knew Dee would be up. Bindi was down the steps and doing her business before Lorelei turned to close her door. She made a mental note to ask Dee about laundry facilities. She was going to have to get those clothes washed before she stunk up the whole apartment.

Bindi was waiting for her as she reached Dee's door, which was still locked. She knocked and waited for a response.

"Is that you Lorelei?" Dee's voice sounded distant.

"It is. Are you okay?" Lorelei tried to door again but it was still looked. Her cell rang, it was a number she didn't recognize. "Hello?"

"Hi, it's Dee. I'm up but having issues with the stairs. There is an extra key in a fake rock in the planter with the pinwheel in it."

"Do you need to go to the doctor?" Lorelei asked.

"Come on in and we can talk."

Lorelei hung up, found the rock and slipped the key out, unlocked the door, placed the key back and hid the rock again. If anyone had been watching, they would have seen her look at a rock and put it back.

Lily met her at the door. She stepped aside and let her out. Bindi chased Lily out in the yard but came back. Lily was still out the yard. "Is this towel by the door to dry Lily off?" Lorelei called up the stairs.

"It is, if you wouldn't mind waiting for her," Dee said.

"Of course not!" She grabbed the towel and used it on Bindi, drying her wiry coat while waiting for Lily to come back inside. Once Lily was in, and both dogs dried off, they all headed upstairs.

"Before you say anything," Dee said as she poured a cup of coffee for each of them, "I'm fine. Just stiff and didn't want to try to navigate the stairs alone. You're here so I wasn't worried." She pulled the creamer out of the refrigerator along with the cream cheese for the bagels.

"And if I wasn't here?" Lorelei asked.

"I would have had to make my way down the stairs so poor Lily could do her business outside. Poor dog would hold it all day if she had to." Dee placed a bagel in the toaster and was splitting open another one, getting it ready to toast.

"Where is the closest laundromat? I need to wash the clothes I was wearing last night at the casino. My whole apartment is going to stink like an ashtray if I don't get them cleaned."

"The closet in the hallway, next to the bathroom, is actually the laundry room. It has a stackable washer and dryer."

"Guess I should explore my new surroundings," Lorelei laughed as she accepted the offered bagel. She spread the cream cheese on it, watching it melt. "I need to stock my own kitchen, eating this way will not be good for me. All the running I do would be useless, and then I'd have to buy new clothes."

"Two bagels will not do you in, and you'll be happy to know I didn't buy these for the house. Jim and Fran asked if I would take some food they knew would go bad before they came home."

"So you're feeding it to me."

"Better than me eating it all on my own." The other bagel popped up. Dee grabbed it, smothered it with cream cheese and walked into the dining room where they sat and ate breakfast. Lorelei refilled their coffee before pulling out her phone.

"I haven't gone through these yet, I thought I would wait until we were together." She purposefully did not mention running into the cop at the casino. She wanted to see if Dee recognized him, to rule him out. She pulled her chair close to

Dee and opened the photo app on her phone. She opened the file dated for yesterday.

"Well, I hope you aren't expecting me to remember him from this view." Dee stifled a laugh as Lorelei saw a large belly contained by a dark blue shirt stressed at its buttons.

"I was trying to get pictures without anyone noticing," Lorelei flicked the screen to get the next photo. This one wasn't much better except the shirt hung loose. "Dang it," she kept flicking through the photos until she finally came across the faces of the security guards that worked last night.

Dee took the phone and slowly scrolled through the photos. "After about the first fifteen photos, you got better at getting faces instead of their belt buckles."

"I got caught by a security guard, he told me to put my phone away and to stop taking pictures."

"What did you do?" Dee asked.

"Went into the restroom and practiced another way to be more sneaky," she said.

"Did you, by chance, get a picture of that one?" Dee kept scrolling through the photos.

"He's one of the last ones. I snapped his picture right before I left for the night."

"I know this guy," Dee stopped and enlarged the photo. "I remember this guy."

Lorelei looked over Dee's shoulder at the picture she stopped on.

"I would hope you would know him," she said, reaching for the phone.

"He's the one who was in the house, I am sure of it, it was him."

Lorelei took the phone from her and looked at the picture of the cop, Michael Smith.

"Dee, this is the cop who was first at the beach, he helped you, and went with you to the hospital."

"Not him, this man here." Dee pointed with a shaky finger to the man who was sitting to the left of Michael "He's the man I saw through the window at Jim and Fran's house!"

"And you recognize the man next to him?" Lorelei asked.

"Of course I do, but I don't know why you'd be taking a picture of him, we know it wasn't him. He wouldn't have been able to leave and come back with his partner."

"I thought you didn't want to talk to the police because you thought someone in uniform might be a part of burglary."

"I am pretty sure it was a security guard uniform the more I think about it. There wasn't a radio attached to the uniform, like you see with cops, or the sheriff. And I remember seeing a radio attached to the paramedic's uniform."

Lorelei rubbed the back of her neck. She had no clue who the man was.

"Where else would there be security guards?" Lorelei asked.

"They're all over. We have two separate casinos, we have security around the college, the art museum, the boat basin, and the other ship yards."

"That's a lot of places to check out."

"We have nothing but time," Dee said.

"But he saw you, so we don't have all that much time. Especially since there has been nothing in the paper about a death from a fall from the bluff. So he knows you're still alive." Lorelei chewed on her lower lip as she was contemplating how she was going to find this guy.

"I have a question," Dee turned toward Lorelei with a wry smile. "Why were you taking pictures of the men playing Black Jack, especially since we knew he couldn't be the one?"

"Maybe I was testing you, to see if you remembered him from the beach or maybe would mistake him for the man in the house."

"You can rationalize that all you want, but you were with him last night, weren't you?" Dee's smile reached her eyes and Lorelei could see she had been quite beautiful in her younger years.

"I was playing a machine, trying to be inconspicuous when I hit a jackpot. Bells and whistles went off and people were cheering."

"Must have been some jackpot, usually they just go about their business."

"It was $4500, and Officer Smith was there in the crowd. And visiting with him while he played cards was a good way for me to get more photos and not be seen."

"And yet you went to the other side of the table to get his picture, which is a good thing, since the man next to him is the one from the house."

"Don't read too much into it," Lorelei mumbled as she took her phone from Dee. "Now I just have to find out who that man is and what he was doing in your neighbor's house. And what did you say was missing?"

"There was art missing off the wall, but I couldn't tell if anything else was missing."

"So maybe I should look at the college's art program and the art museum first," Lorelei was talking to herself as she took her and Dee's dishes back into the kitchen.

"That would be a start, by why the college?" Dee asked.

"Art history, maybe there was something of value that they didn't know they had. I'm not sure. Right now, I going to put my smelly clothes in the wash and take Bindi for a run."

"In this weather?" Dee looked out the window and watched as the rain continued to pour.

"I need to get out there before the wind starts, or I will be dodging branches as well as raindrops."

"The tide is out. Go out and run on Bastendorff Beach. You won't have to worry about the branches, just rain drops."

"I'm going to take Bindi to the beach down below," Lorelei winked at Dee. "I can run the road first then let Bindi run the beach if I feel the need for more exercise. I'll let you know what kind of plan I come up with. Why don't you give me the keys to Jim and Fran's and I'll feed the cat while I'm out."

"That would be helpful," Dee said as she went and got the keys.

Back at the apartment, Lorelei changed into her running clothes. As she put on her shoes Bindi started bouncing, vocalizing her excitement. She knew when her person put on those shoes, it meant she got to go for a run.

Bindi kept bouncing until her person grabbed her purple harness and slipped it on. She then grabbed Bindi's purple raincoat and put it on. She tightened it and then hooked on the matching leash. Bindi stopped at her little boots but when her person didn't stop, Bindi bounced higher. She hated those boots but wore them when she was asked too.

Lorelei warmed up by jogging to the house on the bluff. She let herself in through the back door. After she filled the food dish and gave the cat fresh water, she and Bindi went for their run.

Lorelei ran, with Bindi leading the way, about three miles before heading to the trailhead that led to the beach where she first met Dee. The storm was getting closer and the waves were building. Lorelei watched the surfers as they caught some waves. She wondered if she should pick up surfing. She loved watching them, but the thought of being at the mercy of the ocean wasn't appealing so she let the thought go.

After meeting Dee she realized she didn't have any close friends except her brother and his wife. She never felt lonely. She wasn't the type to share her life with anyone. She had one boyfriend in high school, but he broke up with her because she went to college out of state instead staying close to home so he could continue dating her. She never let anyone dictate what she was going to do. It was hard leaving her twin, Thomas, because they had never been separated, but she knew they both needed to have a life separate from each other. Thomas was now married with a little one on the way, which proved her point.

When the surfers started making their way to the beach, Lorelei went back up the trail.

9

After showering and getting dressed for town, Lorelei sat at the small desk and made of list of what she needed from the store. She needed groceries, and especially laundry detergent to get rid of the cigarette smell. And then she remembered the cash she won last night. She found the sweatshirt and pulled out the wad of cash. She wanted to go the local thrift stores and find some inexpensive trinkets for the place. She wanted to make it her own. She let Bindi out one more time. When she came back in, Lorelei kissed Bindi's nose and told her to be a good girl before leaving for the store.

She drove around the small town, looking for a good place to get some stuff for the apartment. There were a few thrift stores; Goodwill, Salvation Army, and a Hospice store. She decided to hit the Hospice store since she knew many people donated to them from the estate sales. She figured she would find what she was looking for there.

Once in the store she found some throw pillows that were like new. They would match the sofa in the apartment. She also found a nice clock to set on the desk. There were other things but she wasn't in the mood to go through everything in the store.

When she left she noticed a pawn shop just down the road, another good place for getting things cheap. She pulled over and went into the store. She noticed some small statues and noticed a glass sculpture hidden behind them. Lorelei was pretty sure it was a Chihuly. They had a few pieces in the house before Mom sold everything to travel. Neither she nor Thomas were interested in what she had. They both let her do what she needed to start over after Dad.

"How much is that?" Lorelei asked the man in the suit behind the counter. He was startled to see her, and looked in the direction she pointed.

"I just got that in, it's worth quite a bit," he walked over to the piece.

"It's a Chihuly, isn't it?" she asked. He picked it up and carefully placed it in her hands . The colors were amazing and it would go perfectly on the windowsill of the apartment.

"I'm surprised you know what it is, not many people around here know of him." He took the sculpture back from her and placed it behind the other items, hiding it from view again.

"I'm from Olympia, there is a Chihuly museum in Tacoma."

"Oh, so you aren't from here?" he asked. His shoulders relaxed. He leaned toward Lorelei.

"No," she said and didn't feel the need to let him know she had just moved here.

"You will see pieces like for over $5000, but I'm selling it for $3000 ."

"I'll give you $1000 for it."

He raised an eyebrow. "You know what this is worth?"

"I do. And I know that you give pennies on the dollar. I'm surprised to find something like this in a pawn shop."

"Heirloom, and the kid needed money, not some piece of glass."

"And you didn't enlighten him on what it was worth, did you?" Lorelei's cat-like smile caught him off guard.

"Tell you what, I like you." His smile made Lorelei's skin crawl as he boxed up the colorful glass before handing it to her.

Lorelei walked out of the pawn shop with the Chihuly, $1500 less in her bank account, and the need to take a shower. She'd forgotten again about the cash winnings in her purse.

It was worth it. She placed it carefully in the trunk before getting in the car. Next stop was groceries. She stopped at Safeway, on her way home and filled up on food. She thought of getting a package of bagels and cream cheese and decided that as long as she kept running she could splurge on the junk food.

There was a used car lot on her way home. She saw a purple Suzuki Sidekick parked near the road at the end of a long line of cars. She hadn't seen one of these in years. She pulled in and parked next to it.

"You looking for a new ride?" the man asked as he approached her.

"Depends, what can you tell me about this Sidekick?"

"Only had one owner, woman brought it in a few days ago. She decided she needed a vehicle she could get in after her hip surgery."

"So, an old lady had it? Lorelei asked. She grabbed her purse, locked the Honda and tried to opened the Sidekick's door. It was locked.

"I wouldn't say old, but she took a fall down some stairs and since then couldn't ride in it comfortably."

"Would you be willing to give me her name so I can ask about what all she had done with it."

"No, but I would be willing to give her your name and let her make the decision if she wants to contact you."

"Fair enough. Can I take it for a test drive?"

He handed her the keys. She unlocked the door, got in, and started it up. It purred to life. It only had 37,000 miles on it. She rolled down the window and asked, "Did she roll over the odometer or does it really have 37k on it?"

"That's correct. She took it out during the nice weather and kept it in a garage if she wasn't driving it."

Lorelei let out a whistle. "Can you get parts if it breaks down?" she asked.

"No, but there is a garage that I trust with all my cars that can do the work for you."

Lorelei looked around the interior. It was in mint condition, and she swore it still had the new car smell to it even though it was over twenty years old.

She pulled out of the car lot and zipped up the road. She shifted into second, then third and finally to fourth. She had it up to fifty miles an hour before she looked in her review mirror hoping a cop wasn't behind her. She slowed down and did the 35 mph speed limit. She drove farther up Newmark before pulling into McDonald's to turn around and go back.

She parked near her car, got out, and handed the keys back to the man.

"How much to hold this for me? I want to talk to the previous owner before I commit to buying it."

"It's priced at $4995, but I will take a $1000 to hold it."

Lorelei, looked around to see if anyone was watching her before she opened her purse and counted out a thousand dollars in hundreds.

"You've got yourself quite a car here," he said as took the cash from her.

"I will give you $3000 more, in cash, after I talk to the previous owner." She held out her hand to shake on the deal. He hesitated, then shook her hand.

"Follow me," he said then walked back to the office. She fell in step next to him.

"I'm guessing you're going to call her now and have her talk to me?" she asked.

"Yes, I am." He handed her his business card. It read Bob Anderson.

In the office she sat down at the only desk and watched as he picked up the phone and pushed the buttons, calling the previous owner. The nameplate on the desk read Bob.

"Hey Mom, I have a young woman here who is interested in your Sidekick." He was silent for a moment before handing the phone over to Lorelei.

Lorelei got the lowdown on the vehicle and the more she listened, the bigger her grin spread across her face. When she finished the phone call she handed it back to the salesman.

"I believe we have a deal," she said. "Do you take trade-ins?"

Bob laughed, "Yes, I do."

They went back out to the lot and he looked over her car. It had over 250,000 miles on it.

"I can't give you much for a trade in with those miles, how about $500?"

"Works for me," she said.

"Let's go back into my office," he smiled and led her back inside.

She gave him her information, plus $3000 more in cash. He handed $500 of it back, saying he was giving her $500 for her car. He noticed her driver license was still Washington.

"You need to get an Oregon driver's license or I have to charge you Washington State sales tax." Lorelei hadn't lived in Washington since she was eighteen, but kept her state of residence while she was in college in Oregon.

"I'll get it done on Monday and bring it to you. I just found my apartment so I need to take that paperwork to the DMV as well. The title is in the glovebox, along with my insurance information."

"That will work."

Lorelei went back to the Honda, unloaded her groceries and the stuff she got from Hospice, putting them in the Sidekick. She opened the trunk and pulled out the box that held her Chihuly glass sculpture. She took all her information out of the glovebox and gave Bob everything that was pertinent to the car and the sale.

"I'll see you Monday!" she called out as she started the Sidekick again. She put it in gear but before she could leave the lot her phone rang. It was a number she didn't recognize.

"Hello?"

"Is this Lorelei?" a male voice asked.

"Hi Michael," she smiled. "Is this where you ask if I'm available for breakfast tomorrow and I tell you yes and ask what time?"

"So my parents didn't scare you off?" She could hear him laughing on the other end of the phone.

"They did not. I do have to ask if I can call you back, I'm getting ready to pull out of parking lot."

"Just be there around nine tomorrow morning. I will see you then."

"I can do that." Smiling, she hung up the phone and stuffed it in her purse. She didn't want to be tempted to answer it if she was driving.

She pulled out and headed toward the beaches, toward home. She couldn't wait to show Dee her new car. She'd also take a picture of it with the top off and Bindi inside, once it stopped raining, so she could show it to Thomas. She could already see him rolling his eyes at her. She had enough money to buy a brand new vehicle and not put a dent in her bank account. A nice vehicle she could drive up to see him in, but she knew this car would make it to Washington and back home many times to come.

After unloading the car, she knocked on Dee's door. Dee came down the stairs to let her in.

"Come see my new ride!"

Lorelei lead Dee, Bindi, and Lily to her new Sidekick. "Don't you just love it?" She opened the door and Bindi jumped in, ready to go for a ride.

Dee laughed while Lorelei told her all about the car and how she got it.

"You're going to need to keep this in the garage. Let me get you a remote for it so you can just drive right in." Dee went back into the house to retrieved the garage remote while Lorelei played with Bindi and waited for Dee's return.

"Same button for opening and closing the door," Dee said as she pushed the button. The garage door opened and Lorelei drove her Sidekick in and parked near a newer Toyota Prius. She got out, grabbed the box that held the glass sculpture and went to the back door which opened up to the back yard and under the steps to her apartment. She stopped and looked at a large shoe collection that lined the back wall. None of the shoes had matches, just an eclectic collection of boots, tennis shoes, sandals and a few high heels.

As she met Dee in the back yard, with the box tucked under her arm, she asked, "What's with all the shoes?"

Dee started laughing as Lily and Bindi chased a ball she had just thrown.

"I always thought it funny seeing an old shoe laying by the side of the road, and always told myself little stories of how a lone shoe would end up there. And after Harry died, well, I started picking up those old shoes and giving each one a story."

"That is hilarious! I would love to hear those stories some time," Lorelei laughed.

"I have them all written down in a notebook by my desk. Keeps my imagination active," Dee said.

"One of these times you may just find a shoe with a foot inside of it."

"Now that would be a story!"

As they started inside, Lorelei handed the box to Dee, "Can you hold this and I will get the girls dried off," she said as she handed to box to Dee and grabbed the towel to dry Lily and Bindi off. The rain had stopped and blue sky was peeking through the clouds but the dogs were still wet from running in the grass.

"I guess I should have waited to show you my car so you didn't have to do the stairs," Lorelei said as she remembered Dee didn't feel up to walking the stairs this morning.

"After the soak in the tub and Tylenol, I'm doing much better. And it's best to walk the stiffness out anyway. If I sat around, I wouldn't be able to move at all tomorrow."

Lorelei took the box from Dee and carried the box containing the glass sculpture upstairs.

"Wait, I thought I left Bindi in the apartment when I left this morning," Lorelei queried as they made their way to the living room.

"Lily was crying at your door, and I could hear Bindi whining on the other side of the apartment door. I hope you don't mind but I let her out so the two of them could play."

"Thank you," Lorelei said, "I always hate leaving her home alone, but I wasn't sure how long I was going to be gone, and I didn't want her left in the car. We may have stormy weather but it's still warm outside, and I won't leave Bindi in a hot car."

"I was just making some tea, would you like some?" Dee asked from the kitchen.

"I'd love some. I take milk in mine, no sugar."

"I swear we are like two peas in a pod," Dee said coming

out of the kitchen with two cups. She set Lorelei's down on a coaster on the coffee table, next to the box and blew on her own cup, cooling it off.

Lorelei opened the box, pulling out the Chihuly glass sculpture.

Dee's face went pale.

"What's the matter?" Lorelei asked.

"Where did you get this?" Dee asked as she carefully took the glass sculpture from Lorelei.

"Bought it at a pawn shop in North Bend after visiting the Hospice store. I was getting some stuff for the apartment. Why?"

"You know what this is, don't you?" Dee asked.

"Yes, it's a Chihuly. He has a glass museum in Tacoma."

"This sculpture was taken from Jim and Fran's home." Dee's face paled further as she turned it over and looked at the bottom. "Jim commissioned this for their 15 wedding anniversary. The customary gift is crystal but he wanted to do something special. So he did glass and had this made for her. If you look closely at the bottom, you can just see the initials JF next to a 15."

"Well," Lorelei let out a heavy sigh, "now we know where the stolen stuff was taken. But I didn't see any art in there. Mostly it was tools, jewelry, guns, and household junk. How would anyone know about the art and to take it there?"

"I'm not sure." Dee set the sculpture down and stared at it. "How much did you pay for it?"

"He was asking $3000, I talked him down to $1500. It's worth much more than that."

"Yes, it is."

"I wonder how he ended up with it. He was surprised I knew what it was, and he was eager to sell it after he found out I was from Washington."

"So he was willing to sell it to someone who wouldn't

show it off around here."

"What do we do now?" Lorelei asked as she set the piece back on the coffee table.

"I guess the smartest thing would be to call the police, but that isn't going to tell us who broke in."

"I have an idea," Lorelei got up and started pacing. "I have a 'date',". She help up her hands and made quotation marks in the air, "with the cop tomorrow morning."

"A breakfast date? Isn't that a bit unusual?"

"I'm meeting him and his parents at the Pancake Mill. You can't really call that a date."

"How did you manage that?"

"It's complicated," Lorelei said as she walked to the large bay windows to look out toward the ocean.

Dee let out a cough, trying to hide her laughter. She went into the kitchen and after a moment brought out two more cups of tea. She handed one to Lorelei before she sat in one the chairs at the large bay window, keeping her composure. Lorelei took a seat in the chair opposite her and blew on the tea.

"I promise not to laugh anymore," Dee said from over the top of her cup, still trying to hide her smile.

"When he was playing Black Jack, I was with him, trying to get pictures. I felt less obvious since I was with someone. When he finished playing, he said he was meeting his parents at the restaurant. When they showed up, they wanted to know if I would like to join him. I felt it would be rude to say no. Plus, I was hungry."

"And I had dinner here waiting so we could go over those photos."

"I know, but, well, I... I don't know what I was thinking. Maybe if it was just him, but his parents asked me to join them. His parents! I was intrigued. I wanted to know more about him. And to be honest, I had a good time, other than his mom drank a little too much, but his dad was charming."

"And now you are having breakfast with them tomorrow."

"His mom invited me again! What was I supposed to do? Say no? Maybe they didn't want to be alone with him." Lorelei blurted out.

"Did they give you that impression?" Dee asked.

"No," Lorelei mumbled. "They were genuine and we all had a nice visit."

"So, what's your big plan then, with the cop?" Dee decided to let Lorelei off the hook about her breakfast date.

"I thought maybe I could talk to him afterwards. And if it goes well I can invite him here so you and I can talk to him, and show him the Chihuly."

"What do you think he can tell us that we don't already know?" Dee set her cup down on the table between them.

"If I knew that I wouldn't have to ask him questions about it."

"I'm not sure, but if you feel he would be able to help, I'm all up for it." She grabbed her tea and took another sip.

10

Lorelei woke up early, took a shower and got ready for her breakfast date. It wasn't a date, she told herself, but she went through her clothes that had migrated from the bed to the top of her dresser. She put them away as she was deciding what to wear. She wanted to make a better second impression than she had at the casino, where she was in jeans and a sweatshirt, but she didn't have much in the way of a snazzy wardrobe. Something else to put on her list of things to buy; new clothes.

She opted for her standard Levi's and a lavender angora sweater. She went into the bathroom and looked in the mirror. There wasn't much she could do with her long hair, maybe it was time to get it cut, and in a style that was easy to care for. She'd ask Dee if she knew of a salon that could help her out. Getting all the weight cut off would not only make it easier to work with but also relieve the tension from her neck.

She found her eyeliner and her mascara, applied them both and was happy with the effect, accenting her green eyes. She found a clip and pulled her hair back from around her temples back so it wouldn't get in the way of eating. Satisfied she left the bathroom and went to find some shoes. She had a pair of boots with three inch heals that would finish off her ensemble.

Bindi was waiting for her at the door.

"Let's go out, and get you a bit of exercise." She found a ball and took it with her to throw around in the yard.

Bindi bounced after the ball and brought it back for her person to throw for her again. She never tired of this game. The farther her person threw it, the more she got to run. After the fifth time, Bindi brought it back, sat, and waited for it to be thrown again. She heard a door open and ran to greet Lily as Dee made her way over with two cups of coffee in hand.

"I saw you playing and thought I would come visit before you head off," she said, handing one of the cups to Lorelei.

"What are your plans for the day?" Lorelei asked as she threw the ball one more time before taking the offered cup. Bindi and Lily chased the ball. Bindi got to it first, then ran around the yard with it in her mouth while Lily chased her.

"Going to feed the cat, clean his cat box, then come back and probably do some gardening. There isn't much to do in the garden, but I do like to keep the weeds pulled, and it gives me something to do to keep my mind off current events."

"Sounds like a plan," Lorelei said she watched the dogs play.

"Lily needed another dog to play with. I do my best to keep her occupied but sometimes she just needs a more rambunctious playmate," Dee said after a few moments.

"Did you ever think of getting another dog?" Lorelei blew on her coffee before taking a sip. The flavor burst in her mouth, her head anxious for the boost of caffeine.

"One dog is enough for me," Dee said. "The couple that rented the apartment last had a cat. He would sit on the fence and tease poor Lily. She would whimper and cry and the cat ignored her."

"I think Bindi is a better match."

At Bindi's name, she came running up, with Lily behind her, tongue hanging out. Dee picked up the ball this time and threw it. She wasn't able to throw as far as Lorelei. Bindi overshot where the ball had landed allowing Lily to get it first. Now Lily ran around the yard and Bindi bounced around her, barking, trying to get the ball.

"Why don't you leave Bindi with me while you are out? The weather is better and the two can play in the yard."

"What are your thoughts of getting a doggy door put in, in the apartment?" Lorelei asked.

"I've thought about it since most people I rent to have a pet, If you know how to install one, go for it. I'm all for pets, as long as the owners know that when I re-rent the apartment, it needs to be clean so no one knows a pet was there previously."

"I'm guessing the people you rent to have their dogs as a family member so you would never know they were there."

"As luck would have it, you are right," Dee laughed.

Lorelei turned her wrist, looked at her FitBit to check the time.

"I need to get my purse and head out." She finished her coffee, handed the cup back to Dee, and made her way back upstairs. Bindi stopped chasing Lily and watched her climb the stairs. She turned back and started chasing Lily again.

Lorelei came back down with a light blazer, a couple chew toys, and another ball.

"I thought this might keep them occupied." Lorelei tossed the toys out, one at a time and watched both dogs chase after them. Bindi picked up the other ball and chased Lily as they continued to run.

"I'm guessing both will be worn out and asleep by the time you get back," Dee laughed . She picked up the two empty cups that she had set on the small bench by the door. "You go have fun, and let me know what happens."

"I'm going to breakfast, it's not like I'll be gone until bedtime!"

"You never know," Dee said, teasing Lorelei a bit.

"I'll go have fun and I will be back early. I will call if he decides he wants to come over right away. Don't want to spring that on you." Lorelei gave Dee a quick hug before making her way to her car.

She made it to the Pancake Mill, which was just off Highway 101, less than a mile from the casino. She parked and looked around at the other cars in the parking lot. She didn't know what kind of car Michael drove or if he was even here yet. She got out, locked up, and headed for restaurant. There were chairs lining the walls where people were sitting, waiting for a table. The place seemed to be popular. She spotted Michael sitting in a chair furthest away from the door. There was an empty chair next to him. As she made her way to him, he looked up from his phone and sent a brilliant smile her direction.

"I wasn't sure if you were going to be here or not," he said as he stood when she approached. He leaned down, and brushed his lips on her cheek.

"I must admit, this is out of the ordinary for me," she said as she took the empty chair next to his.

"As it is for me." He sat back down and put his phone in a pocket inside his jacket. "My parents will be late. Apparently they had a big dinner group last night and it went on for longer than expected."

"That's okay, I don't have anywhere I need to be anytime soon."

"No plans for the day?" he asked.

"I'm not sure," she said.

"Michael Smith?" the hostess called out. They both stood

at the sound of his name and followed the hostess to a corner booth at the front of the restaurant. She took a seat across from him. He looked out the window which gave him access to the parking lot.

"Can I get some coffee started for you while you wait for the rest of your party?" she asked.

"I'd like that, and with lots of cream," Lorelei said.

"And I'll have the same, along with some water."

"Would you like water as well?" the hostess asked Lorelei.

"I would, that would be great."

"I'll have your waitress bring it right over." She left, leaving them alone.

"You dress up nicely," Michael said.

"Thank you, so do you." Lorelei felt heat rising to her cheeks.

"Didn't mean to embarrass you," he said.

"You didn't. As I said, I'm just new to this."

"You cannot tell me you haven't been on a date before," he said, leaning back in his chair.

"Not in a very long time."

"That surprises me."

"Oh, I've been asked out. I just had too much going on with school and then moving around, trying to find the ideal place to live."

"And you think this is the ideal place?" Michael laughed.

"This was my home when I was little. We moved away when I was about ten. This place has the ocean, beautiful beaches, rivers and lakes, and it's not too far to drive if I need to go to a larger city. Only a two hour drive way," she said. "Plus, I inherited my grandparents house right on the bluff, overlooking the light house."

The waitress brought them coffee and water. She set down a bowl of individual creamers between them. "You're waiting for someone else to arrive?" she asked.

"Yes, there are two more coming," Michael said as he reached for the creamers. He grabbed three and started emptying them into his coffee. Lorelei grabbed four and did the same.

"Can I ask you a question?" Lorelei asked as she stirred her coffee.

"Sure."

"I think I bought a stolen piece of art work from a pawn shop. How should I handle it?"

"I guess it depends. What makes you think it was stolen?" He set his spoon down, took a drink, and waited for her to continue.

Lorelei let out a deep breath, finding the courage to tell him what happened that morning when she found Dee on the beach.

"When I took Dee Brown home from the hospital, I knew something was wrong. She asked me to stay with her that night," she started.

"And you hadn't met her before?" he asked.

"Apparently I had when I was little, and she knew my parents. I haven't seen her in over fifteen years, but she trusted me. She said anyone who would leave their dog with them when they ran off to find help was a good person."

"I guess that makes sense."

"So, I stayed with her and she told me what had happened." Lorelei picked up her spoon and absent-mindedly stirred her coffee again. "She said there was somcone in the house she was watching. She didn't tell anyone because the man was wearing some kind of uniform and she didn't know who she could trust. We went back the next day to feed the cat and to look around. She noticed two painting were missing, but didn't think anything else had been taken."

"Why didn't she call us then?"

"Because she thought it was a cop. She's not so sure now. And I went to town yesterday to get stuff for my new apartment, which is above Dee's garage, and walked into a pawn shop. I saw a Chihuly glass sculpture hidden behind some other stuff behind the counter and asked the man about it."

"A Chihuly?" Michael asked, "what's a Chihuly?"

"And that is the response I am thinking the man at the pawn shop would expect. Dale Chihuly is a well known glass artist with his own museum up in Tacoma. I've been to that museum many times with my parents, we even had some of his art. I recognized it and inquired about it. He seemed surprised I knew what it was. When I explained that I was from Washington area he agreed to sell it. I think it's because he thought since I wasn't from around here, not one would see it."

"Do you have this piece?" Michael asked, giving her his full attention now.

"I took it to Dee's to show her. She said it was stolen from the house she's watching. She turned it over and showed me the initials on the bottom. Jim bought it for Fran on their 15th wedding anniversary. She showed me the JF15 inscribed on the bottom."

"Jim and Fran are the people Dee Brown is house sitting for?" he asked.

"Yes. She saw the man's face as he was walking through the house. When she tried to leave, she tripped over something on the porch and made some noise. She ran for the trail along the bluff and tripped. She slid down and got caught on a root. She's says he saw her, hanging there, and when they made eye contact, she lost her grip on the root. But I think this is why she wasn't hurt, she didn't slide down all at once. She didn't see him look over the edge. She just stayed where she was and kept still."

"And you found her right after that."

"Yes, and when she pointed where she had fallen from, I didn't see anyone up there. We had gone back the next day, to feed the cat. We looked around and found a matchbook from the Mill Casino." Lorelei took another deep breath. "That was when I thought maybe it was a security guard from the casino, since Dee kept mentioning the uniform. So, I told Dee I would go to the casino and see if I could get some pictures, to see if she recognized anyone."

"And did she?" he asked, leaning forward, his interest peeked.

"Yes."

"I'm so sorry we're late!" Ann's voice broke through the conversation. "We stayed up way too late last night. I bet you're hungry waiting for us!"

Ann took the seat next to Michael while his dad sat next to Lorelei.

"I'm so glad to see you again," she said as she reached out her hand to Lorelei, which she grasped in both of hers. "And look at you, you are such a pretty little thing." Her smiled beamed as she looked from Lorelei and then to Michael. "You sure made yourself a nice catch with this one."

"Mom, I told you, we are just friends." It was Michael's turn to blush.

"I'm just glad we get to see you again before leaving town," his dad cut it. He reached over to pat Lorelei's hand. "And I am glad we get to see you both one more time."

The waitress came and took everyones order, and brought coffee and water for Ann and Mike.

"Where are you heading next?" Michael asked.

"Back to Arizona. I am so ready to go back home," Ann said.

The rest of the breakfast was spent listening to the travels Michael's parents had been on since last he saw them. They asked when he would be coming for a visit, since he'd never been to their new home, and if we would bring Lorelei. He politely told them he would see if he could get some time off, but with it being a small town, there weren't many who could cover for him in his absence.

"I've got this," Mike said as he took the check the waitress brought them. "The least I can do."

They left the restaurant and said their good-byes next to a small compact car. "You need help hooking this back up to the motorhome?" Michael asked as his dad got in the car.

"No, I've got it down to a science now. You two go and enjoy the rest of your day."

Lorelei waved as they drove out of the parking lot.

"You have a nice family," she said as he walked her toward her car.

"They are, in small doses. I'm surprised nothing was said about my brother."

"Why do you say that?" she asked as she stopped by her Sidekick, still smiling at her spontaneous purchase.

"He's a hot shot defense lawyer in Chicago, and they expected me to be more like him." Michael turned to the car next to the Sidekick.

"This one's mine," she said, unlocking the door.

"Now why am I not surprised," he laughed.

"I bought it yesterday, when I bought the Chihuly."

"Back to that glass sculpture, and the casino Friday night. What were you doing there, exactly?"

"As I said, taking pictures of the security guards. Can we have this conversation someplace else, and not in the parking lot of a restaurant?"

"You mean like at the station?"

"No, I would like to invite you over to Dee's house. I already told her I was going to talk to you. The reason she didn't let anyone know what she saw was because of that uniform. She didn't know who she could trust. I convinced her she could trust you."

"Thank you," he said, "and, yes, I would like to come and talk with her sometime today."

"Do you know when? So I can let her know?"

"How about I call you when I am on my way?"

"That will work."

They stood staring at each other for an awkward moment. Lorelei thought he was looking at her differently now. She waited one more moment before balancing on her tiptoes to give him a kiss, just to the side of his lips. She could feel the roughness of his stubble on her lips. He reached out to touch her arm, but she opened the door to the Sidekick, slipped in behind the wheel, and left.

On the drive home she tried to figure out what had changed. He had kissed her cheek when she left the casino Friday night, and again when he greeted her at the restaurant this morning. But he kept his distance as he told her good-bye. Was he angry at her for keeping this from him? Or now that she was a witness he had to keep her at arm's length. Her heart sank, just a little, at that last thought. She liked him, she liked his family, but one dinner and one breakfast do not make for a relationship. And she wasn't looking for a relationship. She was happy on her own. She had Bindi. She hadn't even asked Michael if he liked dogs.

11

Michael was on the cell phone to his partner, Amy Holloway, as he made his way to the station. "I need to see you at the office," he said when she picked up on the first ring.

"I'm already here, following up on paperwork, which you forgot to do," she said.

"I have all day, just like you, and I think I have a lead for us with the burglaries that have been happening over the last few months."

"That is a job for the detectives on the case," she said. He could hear her typing at her computer.

"Yes, or it's our foot in the door for that promotion," he replied.

"You're really shooting for one of the next detective openings, aren't you," she said.

"Aren't you?" he inquired.

"Touché!" she said before hanging up.

At the station, Michael parked near the front doors and ran up the steps. He made his way into the station and to his desk. Amy Holloway was sitting at her own desk, next to his.

"We need to go someplace private so we can talk."

Amy looked around the station and saw only one other

officer working. "We can talk here, no one is going to listen in."

"I don't want anyone to walk in while we are discussing it." Michael sat on the edge of his desk, waiting for her replay.

"We can go to the coffee shop down the block, but we will be overheard there, too."

"Humor me and let's just use one of the empty offices." He stood and started down the hall. Amy saved the file she was working on before closing down the program. She signed off her computer before following Michael down the hall.

Once they were inside with the door shut, Michael went and sat at the table and Amy took the seat to opposite him.

"What do you have that we need to keep so hush hush about?"

"Remember the woman who had slipped down the cliff a few days ago?"

Amy pulled her small notebook out and flipped through the pages. "Dee Brown."

"And the woman who found her?"

"Lorelei Silence, what's this about?"

"I ran into her at the casino Friday."

"Brown or Silence?" Amy asked.

"Lorelei, and my parents, who are in town this weekend, ended up inviting her to dinner with us."

"I'm not going to ask how that happened," she said.

"I'm not sure how it happened either, but it did. Dinner went well and my mom proceeded to invite her to breakfast this morning before they left town. My parents were running late so Lorelei and I had time to talk. It seems that Ms. Brown is house sitting for some neighbors. She saw someone in the house. When she tried to get away, she made some noise that may have caught his attention. She tried to hurry, making her way through the trails by the cliff and ended up sliding down. According to Lorelei, the man in the house was in a uniform, which made Ms. Brown afraid to talk to us. And when she tripped and slid part way down the bluff, the man was standing over her before she fell the rest of the way, which explains the footprints we found. They came to the conclusion that it may have been a security guard from the Mill Casino because of a matchbook they found.'"

"They found a matchbook?"

"Yes, near the house."

Amy sat for a moment, elbows leaning on the table, taking all this in, her mind going back to her partner calling Lorelei casually by her first name. "They took it upon themselves to investigate? I don't need to tell you that isn't too smart."

"No, you don't, but because of the uniform Ms. Brown saw, she was afraid it might be an inside job, a cop or something."

"I can understand that," Amy said, leaning back in her chair.

"Also, according to Lorelei," Michael stood up and started pacing, "when they looked through the house they noticed some art work missing off the walls. But Ms. Brown didn't see anything else missing." He stopped pacing, came back to the table, and sat back down. "Do you know who Dale Chihuly is?"

"No, is he the person they think robbed the place?"

"No. He's an artist with a glass museum up in Tacoma. Lorelei is from there so she is familiar with his work. She was shopping yesterday and found her way into the pawn shop in North Bend. She spotted one of Dale Chihuly's pieces hidden behind some stuff on the back counter. She talked pawn shop owner into selling it to her, because she wasn't from around here. She took it to show to Dee Brown, who recognized it as a piece from the house she's been watching.

"So Lorelei talked Dee into meeting me. But I think we need to make it official. I thought if you and I showed up, in uniform, to question them, it would help the investigation and get us on track for that promotion we are both looking for."

"What will that do to your budding relationship with Miss Lorelei?" Amy asked, as she rolled this thought over in her head.

"I'm hoping that when she realizes that I have both her and Ms. Brown's interest at heart, she will forgive me." Micheal stood again and walked around the table as Amy watched him.

"Is she that important to you?" Amy asked.

"I don't know. I don't want to jeopardize what I feel we may be building, but I also don't want to lose this case. We've worked hard for this promotion."

"So let's go talk to them, on the record. And while we do so, you can let Ms. Silence know what is going on. I will keep mum on that part. That is, if you want me to."

"I am not sure what to think. This is new territory for me." Michael wanted answers but not at the cost of misleading the main witness.

"Call her, let her know we will be there, to talk to them both, and to take the sculpture into evidence." Amy stood, letting Michael know this conversation was finished.

"I'll call as we head out." Michael ran his fingers through his short blonde hair.

"And I will do my best to defuse the situation. We need to show up in uniform, to make it official. Let her know we are investigating all leads. She doesn't need to know it's not our case."

"I'll head home and change. Can you pick me up?"

"I can do that," Amy said as she headed for the door. "As long as we keep this official, there shouldn't be any problems. We were first officers on the scene, and Ms. Silence came to you, unsolicited, because she remembered you from the beach when Ms. Brown was found."

"I hope you're right." Michael walked over and open the door. He knew what he and his partner were doing was in the best interest of all parties involved, except maybe the detectives on the case.

He left the station and headed home. Michael put on his uniform and checked himself in the mirror. His six foot two inch frame filled out the uniform nicely. His four days a week in the gym were paying off. And his running five miles a day was a bonus. As he waited for his partner to come pick him up, he called Lorelei.

"It's Michael, I will be over within the next hour, if that works for you and Ms. Brown?" he said, omitting he would be showing up in an official capacity, along with his partner.

"That sounds good. Do you need directions to the house again?" she asked.

"If you don't mind," he said.

She gave directions, letting him know she would be in the house with Dee, and not in her apartment above the garage, waiting for him. Michael pushed the wave of guilt aside as he kept telling himself what he and his partner were doing was right. This was a police investigation into multiple burglaries, and it was the door to his promotion that he'd been working on for the last year.

There was a honk outside his small house. He shifted the curtains by the front door and saw Amy sitting in their official cop car. The markings and lights on the top screamed Cop. One of the reasons he wanted to rise in the ranks to be a detective. His brother may be some hot shot attorney, but that was not the side of the law Michael wanted to be on. He wanted to protect and serve. He wanted to be one of the good guys who protected the innocent. He hated what his brother did.

Jared Smith went to college at seventeen and excelled in his studies. When he became President of the Debate Team, he decided to become a lawyer. Both parents were proud. But Michael asked him what side of the law he would be practicing. Jared told him there was only one side to the law, making sure the guilty are convicted while the innocent go free.

"A prosecutor?" Michael had asked, he was just starting his sophomore year of high school, while Jared was excelling in his junior year of college.

"No way! I want to make sure the innocent have someone beside them when the police and prosecution come after them!" Jared Smith was one of the top defense attorneys in Chicago. And when Michael sees his brother's name in print, he cringes. He subscribed to the Chicago Tribune after Jared became a defense attorney with his own office. It didn't take long before Michael realized Jared was defending small time mobsters. And after a few years, Jared climbed the ranks and had some extremely well known clients who he has been able to keep out of jail. When Michael read those names he knew he was going to be a cop, and put away those type of criminals. Granted, Coos Bay/North Bend was a small area, with their combined population around 26,000 on a good day, but it was a start. Michael had stayed in his home town, where the brothers grew up.

Unlike Jared, he would not forget his roots. He would do his best to arrest the guilty, and help the innocent. He'd been a cop for the last six years, and the last eight months, along with Amy, he'd been studying for his detective badge. Michael believed with this case he and Amy may get their detective shields after all. But is it worth the collateral damage of a young woman like Lorelei? Michael didn't think he would have to hurt her to gain the other, if he played his cards right.

He locked his door before making his way to their official cop car. Lorelei would see it coming from a mile away if she stood at the window and watched. He was hoping she wouldn't. Michael also hoped she wouldn't be upset that he showed up with his partner, in uniform, and proceeded with a formal interview.

They parked in the driveway. Michael and Amy made their way to the gate, opened it, and knocked on the door. He heard dogs barking. After a few moments, Lorelei opened the door with a smile that disappeared when she saw Michael and his partner, in uniform.

"Follow me," she said, without any way of a greeting, and led them upstairs.

12

Lorelei walked ahead of officers Michael Smith and Amy Holloway, who followed her up the stairs to Dee"s living space.

"Dee," she called out, "the police are here."

They made their way to the living room where Dee was sitting at the dining room table, with a cup of tea in front of her. Lorelei gestured for them to sit.

"Can I get you something to drink?" she asked.

"I'm good," Michael said.

"I wouldn't mind a cup of tea," Amy said as she pulled out the chair across from Dee. Lorelei went to make another cup. When she returned, she handed a cup to Officer Holloway and set a glass of water on the table next to Officer Smith. She sat down next to Dee, across from the cops, her back stiff, and wrapped her hands around her own cup.

"After you left this morning, I went back to the station and talked to my partner, and we thought it best if we both came to talk to you," Michael said, matter of factly.

"It would have been nice if you had mentioned this on the phone," Lorelei said coolly.

"We are here now." Michael adjusted himself in the chair.

"Can you show us the glass sculpture?" Amy took over the conversation.

Lorelei stood and went into the living room. She came back with a beautiful glass sculpture which she sat on the table between them.

"What can you tell me about this?" Amy turned to Dee as she pulled out her notebook.

"It's a glass sculpture that my neighbor, Jim, had commissioned by the artist, Dale Chihuly, for his wife, Fran, for their wedding anniversary over thirty yeas ago. It was for their 15th wedding anniversary," Dee rambled.

"And how did you come by it?" Amy turned to Lorelei.

"I bought it at a pawnshop yesterday," Lorelei said.

"Can you tell me what the pawnshop owner said?" Amy asked.

"He was surprised I knew what it was. And when I told him I was from out of the area, he agreed to sell it to me," Lorelei's knuckles whitened as she gripped her tea, not looking at Michael. "He said he just got it in from some kid who had inherited but didn't know what it was worth. After I told him I knew what it was , and that he paid pennies to the dollar, and that I wanted it. He sold it to me. I didn't realize it was from the home that Dee was watching until I showed it to her."

"Do you know if anything else is missing?" Michael asked Dee.

"We believe there were also some paintings stolen." Lorelei answered for her, but she didn't look at him. She kept talking to Amy.

"Any idea which ones?" Amy asked, turning to Dee.

"I'm sorry, I just don't know that much about their art to know what the paintings were, only that they acquired them on their trips abroad. Only reason I know they're missing is because of the empty spaces on the walls." Dee twisted her napkin between her fingers.

"We are going to have to call this in," Amy said to Michael. "If this burglary is related to the others, which I am sure it is, we have to get the fingerprint team down here, and go over the place."

"You said something about photos?" Michael said to Lorelei, ignoring his partner's comment.

Lorelei straightened as she pulled out her phone. She felt gut-punched, unable to understand the man she had dinner with on Friday, and breakfast this morning, to the man who is sitting across from her. Now anger burned inside. She had gone to him, she was the one who was tried to do things correctly, by going to the police. And this is how she is treated?

After unlocking her phone, she opened up her photos as she went around to the other side of the table. She leaned in, between their chairs and showed the photo of the man sitting at the Black Jack table with Michael, from Friday night. What Lorelei also noticed was how Michael was looking at her when she took the photo.

"This is the man who Dee saw in the house?" Amy looked over at Dee, who was nodding her head

"You were at the casino Friday night taking these pictures?" she asked Lorelei.

"Yes. When Dee wasn't comfortable talking to the police, I decided to take pictures, see what I could find. And apparently I was able to find the guy, but it was just dumb luck."

"We need to find out who this guy is," Amy said to Michael. "And is there anyway I can get a copy of that photo?" she asked Lorelei.

"I'll just text it to your partner," Lorelei looked down at her phone, and after a few clicks, sent a picture, and stared at Michael until his phone pinged. She neither blinked or turned away. He finally broke the contact when he retrieved the image. He didn't open the picture, just saw the text was from her.

"I've got it," he said as he stood to leave.

"If there isn't anything else, I will show you to the door." Lorelei kept her composure, and headed for the top of the stairs. She waited for the officers to follow. Amy stayed back to talk a little bit more with Dee, giving Michael a chance to talk to Lorelei alone, to defuse the situation, as Amy had said.

"We need to talk," he said as he walked down the stairs, to the back door. Lorelei looked for the other officer and when she didn't show up, she figured she and Dee were meant to be separated. When they reached the bottom of the stairs, Bindi was already at the door waiting to be let outside.

Lorelei opened the door and Bindi bounded out, coming back with a ball which she placed at Lorelei's feet. She picked it up and threw it across the yard, waiting for Michael to say something.

"I want to apologize to you. If I didn't do it by the book, and someone found out I had been out with you on two different occasions, all the evidence could be tossed out."

"The least you could have done was tell me, not have it sprung on me."

"I didn't have time,"Michael replied.

"Actually, you did. You could have called before your partner picked you up, you could have sent a text on the drive out. You had ample opportunity to let me know. I promised Dee I would only share the information with you, not with all the cops on the force."

"I only shared what you told me with my partner."

"Good for you," Lorelei said as she threw a toy for Bindi. She kept her mouth shut for the rest of the time they were together.

"We need to get back to the station," Amy said she walked

up to them, carrying the box that held the glass sculpture.
    Lorelei said nothing as they walked away.

13

"I cannot believe the nerve of him!" Lorelei said, running her fingers through her hair as she paced Dee's living room. Dee was trying to calm her down.

"Have a cup of tea, and talk to me," Dee said as she sat at the kitchen table.

"I trusted him! I trusted him to help you out. And he brings the calvary!" Lorelei kept pacing, this time around the table, too angry to sit down.

Dee poured her a cup of tea and waited for Lorelei's anger to subside. After a few minutes Lorelei planted herself across the table, in the same chair Michael Smith had occupied, a subtlety that Dee did not ignore.

"I thought I could trust him!" Lorelei huffed as she scooted her chair in.

"And why do you think you can't?" Dee asked.

"He brought his partner." Lorelei reached for the cup, letting it warm up her hands, though they weren't cold.

"And why does that bother you?" Dee asked.

"It was privileged, what I told him."

"And do you want him to lose his job if it comes out he has information that could lead to an arrest for the burglary?"

"No, but he isn't going to get too far. The picture I sent him was one of some guy's belt buckle, not of the guy sitting next to him at the Black Jack table."

Dee hid her smile as she asked, "Why did you do that?"

"I don't know, maybe because I'm angry, maybe because I want to find out who the guy is without his help." She picked up the cup and took a big drink of the fresh tea Dee had made for her.

"That's a bit petty, they have more resources than you do."

"I'm going to find out who he is, without Officer Michael Smith's help." Lorelei stewed in silence as they both drank their tea.

"How are you going to find him?" Dee finally asked after a few minutes.

"I'm going to go to all the places we talked about, and get pictures of security guards."

"Instead of wasting your time, let them find the man instead."

"No, I'm going to do this for you, to keep you out of the picture. I want you safe, and the man caught."

"I'm sure those two who were just here could do that."

"What? Now you want to trust the cops? Especially since he lied to me? He used me, made me think he cared. And it was to get me to open up." Lorelei's anger rose again.

"He didn't know any of that when you saw him Friday, and again Sunday. It wasn't until you confided in him after both those meetings. Give him the benefit of a doubt."

"I will give him nothing!" Lorelei stood abruptly. "How could he do this to me? I though he cared about me! I went to him asking for help and this is how he treats me?"

"Lorelei," Dee said calmly, "he's a cop. He has to follow the rules. Do you want him to lose his job?"

"That's not the point," Lorelei said, still pacing. "I confided in him. He could have at least said he needed to talk to his partner, see what the options were, then let me know. He just comes here, as a cop, and didn't let me know so I could be prepared. To hell with him!"

"That's not fair. He is bound by his oath," Dee said, still trying to calm Lorelei down.

"What about me?" she scoffed.

"He may not have had a choice," Dee said.

"Maybe he didn't, but, he could have told me, before showing up with his partner. Come on Bindi, we have a job to do." Lorelei left Dee's house, with Bindi at her heels.

Back in her apartment, Lorelei made herself a cup of strong coffee in a large to-go cup, took it to the desk that faced the ocean, and sat down. She pulled out a small notebook from the drawer and found a pencil. She started a list of the places she needed to visit. After she finished, she looked it over and prioritized it so she knew where to go first.

She figured the college would be the place to start, but since it was Sunday she decided the museum would be better. She could go to the college tomorrow. The boat basin was on her way so that would be her first stop, and then the ship yard where the new steel boats were being built. The old boat yard was there. She remembered going there with her dad when she was little. He would take her and Thomas to see the boats in the bone yard that had been brought out of the water to be worked on. With the fishing industry geared more to the larger boats, many of the fishermen couldn't afford to work on their boats and they would soon be abandoned.

Lorelei left the list on the desk and went to her room to get a sweatshirt. The wind was cold coming off the ocean but so far the rain had missed them. She would walk the docks, looking at boats and see if she could get any pictures of the security guards. She grabbed her purse and Bindi's harness.

"Let's go!" she called and Bindi came running. Once she secured the harness, she grabbed her coffee, her purse, and locked up. She went down to the garage, used the automatic garage door opener Dee had given her and backed out. She hit the button again. Once she was sure the door was securely closed, she drove toward the boat basin.

The first thing she noticed as she pulled in were all the crab pots stacked around the fish plant. There were pallets filled with pots and buoys in a myriad of colors. Each boat had its own color scheme so they could tell the pots apart from one another out in the ocean. Men were busy working getting the pots ready. It was early November and crab season started in December, barring price wars.

She pulled the Sidekick up to one of the docks, grabbed Bindi's leash and went down to the boats. She walked around, looking at them, taking pictures. She didn't see anyone around who looked like a security guard. She went to the next dock and did the same. She did this all the way around the boat basin and only saw one person she thought worthy of a picture. The man was short, balding and not the one she had seen in the casino. But she took his picture anyway.

She and Bindi walked back to the Sidekick, got in, then left the boat basin, heading for the bone yard on the other side of the Charleston bridge where the derelict boats rested. She again took Bindi for a walk, looking for anyone who resembled the man she had seen sitting next to Michael Friday night.

The thought of Michael Smith made her stop. She was angry with him, but more angry at herself for letting herself think maybe there was something between them. She didn't have time for a man. She needed to get settled in, get her house repaired, and find a job. She didn't want to rent and throw her money away, making someone else rich with her hard earned money. Okay, she thought, not hard earned, not right now, but when she was working it would be her hard earned money. Which meant she also needed to start looking for work soon. She couldn't live on her mom's hand outs for the rest of her life, she needed to make her own way. It's what she went to college for. But she didn't get a degree that would set her up in life with a good job. Maybe she should look into going back to school. She shook her head as the thought of going back to college entered her head. She didn't want to go back to school. She just wanted to get a job and have a nice home here.

Her cell phone rang. She looked down and recognized Michael's number. After a few rings she decided not to answer it and silenced it, making it go to voicemail. He must have finally opened her message and saw it was the wrong picture. Let him stew for a while, she mused. She'd call him back, or maybe just text hime the correct picture later so she didn't have to talk to him. She didn't want to talk to him. She knew she wasn't being fair. She also knew it wasn't Michael who asked her to dinner, and breakfast. It was his mom. But would he have asked her? Lorelei didn't know, at that the moment, decided it would be best to put those thoughts on the back burner. She had a job to do.

The boats in the bone yard were in various stages of decay. Some were so far gone they had a large X painted on their hulls, marked for destruction. These boats had served their owners well and were left to be destroyed. There wasn't much need for the small fishing trollers anymore. The large steel boat with their large nets had taken their place.

She walked to the end of the road and turned to walk where the new boats were being built. These large boats were the future of fishing in this little town. She saw a couple men talking next to one of the few boats on dry dock. She went up to them.

"Hello?" she said as she neared.

"Is there something I can help you with?" the older man asked. He was in his late fifties, Lorelei guessed, dressed in dirty blue jeans and a plaid flannel shirt.

"I am wondering if either of you know this man?" She pulled out her cell phone and showed the two men the picture from the casino. "I think he's a security guard but I don't know where he works."

"What'd he do?" the younger man asked. He was dressed in jeans and a tattered sweatshirt.

"I am looking for him for my aunt, he had helped her with a flat tire and she didn't have a chance to thank him. I told her I would see if maybe he worked down here since it was close to the bridge where she got the help."

"How do you have a picture of him on your phone?" The older man pulled a toothpick out of his mouth and pointed at the photo with the chewed end, "Seems to me you already know where to find him."

"Um... well... see the man next to him? That's my boyfriend. He and I were at the casino when I took this. When I showed my aunt the picture, she recognized the man next to him as the man who helped her."

"Then maybe you ought to go back to the casino," the younger man said before starting back up his conversation with the older man, dismissing Lorelei. She waited a moment before giving up and walked away.

Back at her car she cursed herself for being so stupid. That was the lamest excuse, and they saw right through her. She needed to figure out a better way to find the man in the picture. And if she was going to ask questions, they needed to sound legitimate. She started her car. Her cell phone rang again. It was Michael. Officer Michael Smith, she reminded herself, the cop. She sent it to voicemail again and headed into town.

Lorelei circled the block until she found an empty parking spot at the back of the museum and parked.

"You have to wait in the car this time. Not all places are pet friendly, you know." She ruffled the fur on Bindi's head before she grabbed her purse and headed into to Coos Art Museum. The Mairtime exhibit was featured, and it had works from Pacific Northwest artists. As she went through the large gallery, she saw paintings, photographs, ceramic sculptures, along with metal works. There were also some glass works, but nothing compared to the stolen Chihuly she had bought.

She slowly walked around looking at the art. There was so much to take in. It brought her back to her art classes in college. She had taken photography and was pretty good at it. Some of the photos of the coast were filled with amazing colors taken during sunsets. The more she looked the more she wanted to take photos like these. Or at least along these lines. She had a different eye than the photographers who had their works hanging here.

"Do you have any questions?" a voice asked from behind her.

"These are amazing!" Lorelei said as she turned to the man behind her and looked into the eyes of the man from the photo.

He looked up at the photo she was standing in front of and didn't see the color drain from her face. "There are so many talented photographers. It's always hard to choose which pictures to hang for this show."

"I can imagine," she squeaked out. She turned from him as she stuffed her shaking hands into her pockets.

"Would you like me to show you around?"

"Thank you, but I'm okay." She walked away, slowly, as she pretended to look at the other art. She needed to leave but didn't want to run out. It would look suspicious and she didn't want to draw anymore attention to herself. She also needed to make sure it was him so she decided to get a picture of him somehow.

Her heart raced as she walked around the rest of the exhibit. She took a chance and turned back to the man. He was still looking at the photo she commented on, his hands clasped behind his back, relaxed. She could see his reflection in the glass covering the photo as she carefully made her way to a sculpture near him. She pulled out her phone, held it like she was reading a text message and opened the camera app. Trying to remember the angle she needed, she adjusted the phone trying not to be obvious. She kept her thumbs moving as if texting before tipping the phone to take a picture of man's reflection.

"I can't seem to get any reception," she muttered aloud, hoping he would hear and think she was trying to get a few bars as she kept moving the phone around.

"No cell phones allowed in here," he said, turning to her.

Startled, Lorelei jumped, then tried to recover by answering, "Oh, I'm sorry, I'm meeting someone and I am trying to let them know where I am."

"Please take it outside, and make your call there," he said. "Now if you will excuse me." He made his way to another patron in the another part of the gallery.

Lorelei stuffed her phone in her purse and thought it wise to leave while he was occupied. She slipped out and down the stairs to the street where she finally let out the breath she hadn't realize she was holding. She looked around and saw people walking on the sidewalk across Anderson Street. She looked down the street and didn't see anything. She walked down the block, turned the corner and headed behind the large building. Bindi started barking as she dug for her keys in her purse. Foot steps sounded behind her, but before she could turn something wrapped around her neck, dragging her backwards while cutting off her air. She tried screaming but no sound came. The last thing she remembered was the sound of Bindi's bark.

14

Michael tried Lorelei's phone one more time before grabbing his jacket. He and Amy had remained at the station all day and through part of the evening, trying to figure out what was happening with the burglaries. They had the glass art they had taken from Lorelei. Plus the statements from Dee Brown and copies of the reports from the previous burglaries.

"She still not answering?" Amy asked.

"No." He let out a long sigh as he hung up when he got her voicemail again. He wasn't going to keep leaving messages. She would already see he'd called four or five times. He was heading to the door when he heard a call come in from another officer's radio who had just come off duty.

"We have a call for an abandoned vehicle left at the Art Museum, with a little dog left inside. It's been there all day. Someone needs to go check out a purple Suzuki Sidekick in the back parking lot."

Michael stopped and turned toward Amy, "That's Lorelei's vehicle."

"What makes you say that?" she asked as she stood, putting her hands at the small of her back and stretching.

"My gut," he said as he headed out the door with Amy

following. They took his car and made their way the three blocks to the museum. There was an officer there, looking over the car as they parked and exited Michael's car. He could see the little dog in the car scratching wildly at the window. The officer was talking to the dog while looking at the locks.

"Get it unlocked," Michael said as he approached. "Hey girl, we'll get you out of there, hang on."

"You know this car?" the officer asked.

"Yes, the owner is a witness to the burglaries that have been going on in the area."

They worked together and got the Sidekick unlocked. Michael picked up the little dog and held her close as she struggled to get away.

"What do you think happened?" Amy asked, stroking the dog's fur trying to calm her down. She took the leash from the car and hooked it to the halter. She looked at the tags on collar and found an ID tag with the little dog's name; Bindi. Amy set her on the ground. First thing Bindi did was go to the bathroom. She had been in the car for close to nine hours. When she finished, she pulled at the leash, pulling Amy toward the back door to the museum. She scratched at the door and started whining. As Amy picked her up Bindi nipped at her and started scratching at the door again.

"Get someone over here who can open that door," Michael said to the cop who had been first to arrive. "I want someone to check out the museum, see if the missing woman is inside."

"How do you know we have a missing woman?" the cop asked.

"Just do it!" He gave the office a detailed description of Lorelei, and Amy noticed he left nothing out.

"We need to get to Dee Brown's house and find out what Lorelei was doing," Michael said, turning to Amy. They went back to his car and got in, Amy held Bindi tight as she struggled to get away again. Michael pulled out and sped toward Charleston. It took them ten minutes to get to Dee's, but in Michael's mind it took forever.

Dee was startled by the pounding on her door. She carefully made her way down the stairs to see who was there. She didn't open the door but called out, "Who is it?"

"Ms. Brown, Officers Smith and Holloway, we were here this morning." Michael said.

Dee opened the door and saw them standing there with a frantic little dog in Amy's arms.

"Bindi!" Dee reached for the little dog but she missed as Bindi jumped and took off up the stairs to the apartment. "I don't understand, why do you have Bindi? Where's Lorelei?"

"That's what we came here to find out," Amy said as she made her way into the house, followed by Dee. Michael followed Bindi up Lorelei's steps and tried the door. It was locked. He didn't trust Bindi to leave her alone so he scooped her up and took her to Dee's. Once the door was closed he let her go. The little dog took off up the stairs to the main living area and started sniffing around the room, where the three of them found her as they made their way into the living room. Dee fell into her chair, wild eyes searching for answers as she stared and Michael and Amy.

"Do you have keys to the apartment?" Michael asked.

"Yes, they're hanging by the door. Can you please tell me what's going on?" Dee hands trembled as she help a small pillow in her lap.

"We found Lorelei's car outside the museum. She was no where to be found." Amy pulled out her little notebook. "Can you tell me what time she left today? And where she was going?"

"She was upset. She didn't like the fact that Officer Smith brought you with him this morning. She was under the impression he was coming over in an unofficial capacity. She said she was going to find out who that security guard was without your help." A tear slid down Dee's cheek. She wiped it away with the back of her hand. "I tried to explain to her that he was only doing his job, and that the two of you had more resources than she did and to leave it to you. She left about a half hour after you left this morning back went back to her place. Then I saw her drive away around noon."

Michael looked at his watch. "It's almost 10:00, which means she could have been missing for at least eight hours.

"Do you know where she went?" Amy asked again.

"Just that she was going to find the guy. She didn't share her plans with me." Now the tears streamed down her cheeks. Amy pulled a tissue from the box on the coffee table. She handed it to Dee who wiped her wiped her eyes, dried her cheeks, and dabbed her nose.

"We need to get into her apartment," Michael kneeled in front of Dee and grabbed both her hands in his.

"This is all my fault," Dee sobbed, "If she hadn't found, me none of this would be happening."

"And if she hadn't found you, you could have died," Michael said gently.

"I know, but..." Dee started.

"No buts, and don't think like that. Now, I need to get into Lorelei's apartment. Do I have your permission?" he asked.

Dee nodded.

Michael stood.

"I'll stay with her," Amy said.

Michael ran down the stairs. He grabbed the keys hanging by the door. Bindi made it out the door before he could grab her. She ran up the stairs to the apartment again, trailing her leash behind her. Michael got to the top and tried each key until he found the right one. He opened the door and Bindi darted inside, searching the small living space, looking for her person. As she disappeared into the bedroom, Michael looked around. He went to the desk and looked at the list Lorelei had written early. She had the museum marked with a #1. He didn't know if she had gone anywhere else first, and then was followed to the museum where she was abducted.

"Abducted." The word sat heavy on his lips as he looked around. Maybe she was just having dinner at one of the restaurants in the area, he thought. No, she wouldn't leave Bindi sitting in the car like that. If Michael knew anything about Lorelei, it was she loved her little dog and would not leave her alone, locked in a vehicle all day.

Taking Bindi with him, he went back to Dee's to talk with his partner.

"We need to go talk to the owner of the pawn shop," he said as he entered the room.

"I'll get the address," she said as she stood up. "It's in one of the reports on my desk."

"Can we leave Bindi with you?" Michael asked Dee who was still wiping away tears.

"Of course," she said.

"I would advise not letting her outside without a leash. She will take off trying to find Lorelei."

"The yard is secure, she can't get out."

"But I don't think you can get her to come back once she's out. She'll stay on the steps of the apartment. And by the way you are moving, the less steps you have to do the better."

"Okay," Dee said as she absently rubbed her knees.

"We're going to find her, and bring her home," Michael said gently.

"She's in this mess because of me, she wanted to help, to find this man." Lily sat at Dee's side, head resting on her leg. Dee rubbed the dog's ears. Bindi was downstairs whining at the door, trying to get outside. Dee stood, went into the kitchen and put some dog food in the dishes she had set out for the dogs. She called Bindi firmly and the little dog obeyed. She sat next to the food dish, staring at Dee before looking back down at her food. She laid down and rested her head on her front legs, whimpering as she stared at the bowl of untouched food.

"We need to go," Amy told Michael as he pulled a card from his wallet.

"Write your number down, and I will personally call you when we find her," he said as he handed the card to Dee. She wrote her number down with a pen she found on the counter then handed it back. Michael stuffed the card in his back pocket. "I will be calling you." He turned and followed Amy out of the house.

"The pawn shop is owned by Alex Hastings and his wife Cheri. I have their home address." She gave it to Michael as he tore out of the driveway, hitting speeds well above the 40 mph speed limit on the road.

"Call the officers who were on the scene at the museum. Tell them what we know, and have them meet us at Hastings's house. Tell them we may have a kidnapped woman inside and they need to keep their sirens off. I don't want them to panic before we get there."

Amy placed the call, alerting the officers to the situation and how it was to be handled.

"Should I call the detectives who are working the burglaries?" she asked as they made their way into North Bend.

"I think it would be best," he said as he searched the house numbers on the street Alex Hastings lived on. He saw a cruiser parked in front of a dark home, the officers were standing next to the car. He pulled up behind them and got out.

"We believe that Alex Hastings and his wife have a partner in the robberies and that they've got something to do with the disappearance of the witness, Lorelei Silence," Michael said as he got out of his vehicle

"We've walked around the house, there's no one here. The garage is empty," one of the officers said.

"Where would they take her?" Michael turned to his partner.

"We need to find Alex Hastings to figure that out," Amy asked.

"We need to find out who the man at the casino is," Michael said as he turned back to his car. "We need to see if we can look at the security footage from Friday night."

"When the detectives get here, let them know where we've gone," Amy told the officers before she followed Michael to the car.

"What are you going to tell them to get them to show us the security footage? We don't have a warrant," Amy said.

"I'm going to let them know a woman's life is at stake and we don't have time for games. I'm not asking for personal information, just the picture of the man." He ran his free hand through his hair as he drove the two miles to the casino. "Why didn't she just send me that picture?"

"It'll be okay, we'll find her." Amy held on to the car door as Michael took a corner too fast. The tires screeched but kept their traction.

Michael pulled up to the front of the casino and jumped out of the car and ran inside.

"You can't park here!" a young valet yelled out.

Amy turned, pulled her badge, "Police business," she said then followed Michael. She found him talking with a security guard.

"We need to talk to the head of security, please," Michael said as he showed his badge to the woman who stood in front of him.

"You're talking to her," the woman said as she held out her

hand, "Missy George." Michael accepted the offered hand.

"I'm Officer Michael Smith, and this is my partner," he turned to Amy, "and this is Officer Amy Holloway. We are looking for a man who was here Friday night playing Black Jack. He was at that table," Michael pointed to the table he had sat at, "between six and seven that evening."

"Very specific," Missy George said.

"I was there, and we are looking for the man who was sitting to my left."

"What'd he do? Cheat? Steal some of your chips?" Missy crossed her arms across her large frame, not moving.

"We think he is involved in a string of burglaries, and the woman who ID'ed him has gone missing. We don't have a name, we need to get his picture out and find out who this man is."

Missy George took them to the back room of the casino, where all the security camera are set up.

"Listen up!" she called out to the people in the room, "I want to know if any of you worked the camera for Black Jack table 3 Friday night." Missy turned to Michael and Amy, "It'll be faster this way, instead of going through all the footage from that night."

"I appreciate your help," Amy said.

"Miss George, I have that camera," a skinny kid with acne all over his face said. "I was working it Friday too."

"Is he old enough to be here?" Amy asked Missy as they made their way to the computer the kid was working on.

"Only need to be eighteen to work here, just can't go out on the floor and gamble."

The skinny kid gave up his seat to Missy George as she started going through the computer. She pulled down a menu and input the date and time they were looking for. The screen went black for a moment and then Michael appeared on the screen, and the man they were searching for was seated next to him.

"That's him," Michael said as he turned to Amy.

"That's Daryl Miller, he's a regular here. Comes in, spends big, wins bigger. We keep an eye on those players, the ones who bet large and win large."

"I don't suppose you have an address for him," Amy asked.

"For that, you need a warrant, my hands are tied on that rule, I wish I could." Missy George led back out onto the main floor of the casino.

"Thank you for what you were able to give us, we can get that information," Amy said as she extended her hand. Missy shook it with a firm grip.

15

The room was dark, no light came through the blindfold that covered Lorelei's eyes. The smell of mildew was faint in the air. Her shoulders ached from having her hands tied behind her back as she sat on the hard chair. She could make out voices from the other room. She wasn't sure but she thought she recognized the voices of both men. One from the pawn shop, the other from the museum. There was a woman's voice that mixed in. The woman was angry, her voice rising above the two men.

"What were you thinking?" she yelled.

"She knows who we are, and keep your voice down," one of the men said. Lorelei couldn't make out which one. The voices lowered and she couldn't make out what they said next. She pulled at the ropes that held her to the chair, twisting her hands and wrists, in the hopes of loosening the knots.

Rubbing the blindfold with her shoulder, she tried to maneuver it off her eyes. She didn't know where she was, where he had taken her. With one more effort, she moved the blindfold enough to see under it with her right eye. Light spilled in from under the door and she could just make out a bunch of boxes stacked around the door. Was she in the pawn shop's back room? She didn't know.

Lorelei worked the blindfold with her other shoulder as pain wracked her body. Her shoulders burned from being pulled behind her back. She needed to get away, to escape before they decided what to do with her. Her thoughts went to Bindi who was locked in the Sidekick. The only thing she was grateful for was that it was overcast and Bindi would not be in a hot vehicle. Oh Bindi, I'm so sorry, Lorelei thought as her heart sank. Please let someone find you.

Footsteps approached the door and the knob turned. Lorelei dropped her head down, her chin resting on her chest. The door opened and light filled the room. She kept her head down, trying to control her breathing, hoping they would think she was still passed out from whatever they had given her. She didn't know how long she'd been out. She didn't know if it was still Sunday.

"She's still out," Daryl Miller, the man who had taken her from the museum, said. "We have another hour or so, then we have to figure out what to do with her. We can't keep her here."

"What do you suggest we do?" the woman snapped back at him. "It's your fault we're in this mess."

"Baby, don't start layin' blame or we won't get nothing done," the man from the pawn shop said.

"Daryl's the one who brought her here!" she snapped back.

"Dammit! No names!" Lorelei assumed it was the man from the museum as he yelled back at her.

"You said she was still out so what does it matter?" she said.

"Because if she hears us, she will be able to tell the cops who we are."

"Who said she's going to talk to the cops?" Lorelei could hear things being tossed about in the other room. Were they in the pawn shop?

"When she's found, she'll be singing like a canary," the man from the pawn shop said.

"If she's found," the woman said.

Panic-stricken, Lorelei struggled with her bonds again once the door was closed. Were they going to kill her?

"What do you mean *if*? Of course she'll be found, but we need to be out of town before that happens."

"I'm not leaving any witnesses behind. We came too close to being caught in that last town. I am not going to let that happen again," the woman said coldly.

"We're thieves, Cheri, we are not about to take a life," the pawn shop owner said.

"I thought you said names!" the woman screamed.

Silence filled the air.

"All we have to do is leave her someplace and let nature take over. She won't last long," Cheri said.

"What's wrong with you?" We can't kill her," the man who had snatched Lorelei growled.

"We won't, the elements will. We can dump her on one of the side roads as we leave town. Now go get the cash we have stashed. And you need to get your money, wherever you keep your share hidden," she said, "and meet back here at midnight."

Footsteps sounded on the old wood floor, then faded away before the slam of a door brought Lorelei to action. She didn't know how much time she had to get out of there. She pulled and twisted then stopped. She moved her legs, they weren't tied to the chair. She rocked the chair back and forth until it tipped over. She smashed her head on the wood floor and laid there, weak with fear but she needed to get out of there, wherever there was.

Lorelei moved and found she was not tied to the chair, her hand were still bound but she wiggled until the back of the chair was no longer between her hands and her back. She curled into a ball and pulled her hands down and pulled until she could pull her legs through. With her hands in front of her, she pushed up her blindfold off her head and looked around. She could see the street lights' glow under the door. Using her teeth, she pulled on the knots, untying her wrists. She rubbed the stiffness out of her shoulders, got up and went to the door. Slowly, she opened it and heard voices near. She quickly pulled herself back in the dark room. She felt around until she found something heavy she could use as a weapon. Whispering voices entered the pawnshop. She pushed herself against the boxes near the door and waited. The door to the back room opened and she swung her club high, as hard as she could as the body came into the room. She heard the crunch as it connected with the person's face. She ran out the door but was grabbed from behind.

"Let me go!" she screamed as she struggled against the bear hug that held her tight.

"Lorelei! It's me!"

Lorelei shook in Michael's arms as a sob escaped her. He turned her around, keeping his arms around her

"They are coming back," she cried, "they plan to kill me!"

Michael held her tight, stroking her hair. "You're safe now, no one is going to hurt you, I've got you."

Her knees buckled. Michael caught her and helped her into the chair that sat behind the counter. He knelt down in front of her, pushing her hair out of her face. She looked at him, blood spilled out of the cut above his eye.

"I though you were one of them, I didn't mean to hurt you," she sobbed

"That's okay, I'll survive," he said as he reached for her hands.

His partner was at his side with a towel for his head.

"How did you find me?" she asked, looking from Michael

to Amy.

"We came here hoping to find answers to where they took you," Amy said as she placed a hand on Lorelei's shoulder.

"I was so stupid, I should have sent you the guy's picture, I shouldn't have gotten so angry," she said, her body still shaking.

"It's over," Michael said as two men in uniform came in the building. "We've got her, she's okay."

Michael pulled his cell phone out, then dug in his back pocket for his business card. He dialed the number on the back.

"Hello?" answered a familiar voice.

"Ms. Brown? I have someone here who wants to talk to you." Michael said. He handed the phone to Lorelei.

"Hello?" Lorelei said.

"Oh my god, you're safe!" Dee said through tears.

"I'm safe," Lorelei said. "Is Bindi with you?"

"Oh, Honey, I've been so worried!" Dee answered.

"I'm okay, I'm just worried about Bindi, is she there with you?"

"Bindi and Lily are curled up in Lily's bed. Took a little bit to settle her down, but she's sleeping now."

"I don't know when I'll be there. Can she stay with you tonight?"

"Of course she can. Just come home safe and sound. I'll be staying up for a while, so if the lights are on, please come see me," Dee said.

"I'll see you when I get there." Lorelei handed the phone back to Michael.

"Ms. Brown, we have her and she's safe. We will be taking her to the hospital to get checked out, and if she's up to it, to the station to go over her statement while it's still fresh in her mind. We will have her home in the morning," he told Dee.

"Okay, she has a key, she can just come here, I'll have the

couch made up for her."

"When are they coming back?" Michael asked Lorelei as he put the phone away.

"They said they would meet back here at midnight, but I don't know what time it is. There are three of them. It's the woman who wants me dead. She said she doesn't want to leave anyone behind who can identify them."

"A woman?" Amy asked.

"Yes, I think it's the pawn shop owner's wife and they said to meet back here after they get all their money, and then they would take me with them when they leave town." Lorelei couldn't calm herself, talking a mile a minute.

"Cheri Hastings, Alex's wife," Michale said.

Amy picked up a small purse that sat on the counter. "Is this yours?" she asked Lorelei.

"Yes," she said as Amy handed her the purse. She opened it and saw her wallet and cell phone still inside. "They didn't take anything."

"We need to leave it there," Amy said, taking the purse back from Lorelei.

"Why?" Lorelei asked.

Michael looked at Amy and the officers, then back down to Lorelei.

"Would you like to help us catch them?" he asked her.

She rocked back and forth, hugging herself, and said, "I don't know how I can help. I don't know where they went and I didn't see her. Just heard her talking, yelling and screaming at them. One of them is named Daryl, I didn't hear any other names."

Michael explained to her what they were going to do, and it meant that Lorelei had to go back to the chair, in the back room, in the dark.

"I won't tie you back up, but we need to put the blindfold back on. I'll have the ropes around your hands, but they won't be tied. We will be in the room here with you, Amy and I, and the officers will be waiting outside, out of sight. Do you think you can do that?"

"And you will be here with me the whole time?" Lorelei asked.

"Yes. I'll take your spot behind the door where you were hiding. And Amy will find a spot on the other side. We won't let anything happen to you. But we need to get set up now since they could be here anytime."

Amy walked over to talk to the other cops. Michael stood and helped Lorelei to her feet before taking her back to the room where she had been held. After the door was closed, Michael felt around for a light, turned it on. A single lightbulb hung from the ceiling casting faint shadows in its dim light. He surveyed the back room. He grabbed the overturned chair and sat it back in the middle of the room. Lorelei tentatively took her seat. She placed her arms around the back of the chair as Michael loosely wrapped the rope. She had to hold the rope to keep it from slipping off. He knelt in front of her again, holding the blindfold.

"I'm going to be standing right over there, and Amy will be behind those boxes." He pointed to a stack of boxes next to the far wall. "They will not touch you, ever again, I promise."

"Okay," Lorelei whispered.

"I need to put this back on," he said as he slipped the blindfold back over her head. He felt her body tense as he covered her eyes. "Bindi is safe at home with Dee, focus on that, and we will get you there as soon as this is over."

"Thank you." Lorelei broke down crying again.

"It's because of Bindi we are here. We heard the call about an abandoned dog, left in a purple Sidekick, as we were leaving the station. And I knew it was you." Michael wiped the tears streaming down Lorelei's cheeks with the cuff of his jacket. It was rough on her face. "I'm sorry I don't have a handkerchief of something."

"That's okay." It came out as a sob. "Guess I know what to get you for Christmas."

Michael leaned in and kissed her cheek, then gently brushed his lips across hers, tasting the salt from her tears. "I'm going to leave you now, but I will only be a few feet away. And we need to stay quiet, can you do that for me?"

"I think so." She took a deep breath, trying to calm herself.

Amy came back into the back room, turned out the light and made her way behind the boxes as Michael took up his spot behind the door. They could hear Lorelei's quiet sobs as they waited.

After fifteen minutes, voices sounded outside the door in the pawn shop.

"Have you got what we need?" a male voice asked.

"Everything but the woman," another male voice answered.

"Why can't we just leave her here?" the first voice asked.

"Because Cheri will have your head on a platter if you don't do as she says," said the second voice. "She told us, no witnesses. We'll take care of her on our way out of town."

The door to the back room opened. A tall figure approached Lorelei as she sat in her chair. He didn't bother with the light. Lorelei felt someone tugging at the ropes behind her.

"Please, just let me go. I won't tell anyone what happened."

"Sorry," the male voice said, "we can't leave any witnesses behind."

"But I didn't see anything!" Lorelei cried.

"You saw Daryl, and that is enough," the voice said.

"But I don't know who he is!"

The lights came on as Michael and Amy came into view. "But we know who you are," Amy said.

At that moment, the sound of the cops coming into the pawnshop could be heard at the front of the store.

"And it seems your partner is being confronted as we speak," Michael said as he took Alex Hastings into custody.

"I"m not saying anything! I want a lawyer!" Alex yelled.

"And we will make sure you, Daryl and your wife have one," Michael said, close to Alex's ear as he handcuffed him.

"I don't know what you're talking about. There's no woman with us," Alex said as they took him from the room.

Other police cars arrived at the scene. They took Alex Hastings and Daryl Miller into custody and loaded them into the awaiting cop cars outside. Lorelei stood and watched with Amy and Michael on either side of her.

"There was a woman," Lorelei said to both Michael and Amy. "I didn't see her, but heard her."

"And her name is Cheri Hastings." Amy pulled out her notebook and started writing. To Michael she said, "I will see what I can find out once we get back to the station."

"What happens now?" Lorelei asked.

"You and Dee will be contacted by either the police or the DA and give a statement. You will need to personally identify each of them, to the best to you knowledge, and the DA will take it from there," Michael said.

"But neither of us can identify the woman, and now that she's gone, what will happen?"

"We'll worry about that when the time comes. Right now, I want to get you to the hospital, have you checked out, then get you home, safe. After that, Amy and I are going to get started on making sure these guys go away for a long time."

"Dee can identify one of the men. The one she saw in the house she was watching. And I saw both men, but I didn't see who kidnapped me or who was in the other room."

"You can identify them by voice. And you can corroborate Dee's testimony by what you heard," he responded.

"Yes, I can. Those voices will haunt my dreams for a long time."

"Let's get you to the hospital," Amy interrupted.

"Okay," Lorelei said, leaning on Michael as he helped her to the front of the pawn shop.

16

Dee didn't like waiting. She spent her time pacing, slowly, waiting to hear from Lorelei or Lorelei's cop friend. How long did it take to bring her home? It shouldn't take too long at the hospital, she was sure of that. And Dee couldn't see the cops keeping Lorelei at the station too long after what she'd been through. She looked at the wall clock and saw it was getting close to two in the morning. Maybe they weren't bringing her home, or maybe there was something wrong when they took her to the hospital.

Dee's pacing had both Lily and Bindi on edge. Bindi's little body shook. Her person left her in a strange car that wasn't theirs, then left with some strange man, leaving her stranded in the strange car. The man and woman that had brought her home had a familiar smell but Bindi didn't trust them. Once they left her with Lily, she was a bit more relaxed, but still needed her human. She was never left overnight on her own. Her human would be here anytime. So Bindi stayed close to Dee as Dee continued to pace back and forth in front of the large bay windows.

Lights from a car drove past Dee's driveway, but didn't turn in. She went into the kitchen, grabbed a small glass from the cupboard and poured herself a double shot of whiskey. She carried it back into the front room and continued her pacing, forgetting that she was holding the glass. Another set of headlights were coming down the road and she saw the turn signal come on before the car pulled into the driveway. Dee made her way carefully down the stairs, still carrying the glass of whiskey. She was sore from the tumble down the cliff as the Tylenol had worn off hours ago. As she got to the back door, she heard the gate latch and footsteps approaching the house. She opened the door, and standing on the steps was a short, round woman with black hair pulled tight in a pony tail, and in her hand was a gun. Dee didn't know anything about guns other than they were dangerous and you never want to have one pointed at you.

"You and I are going to have a little talk, while we wait for your roommate to come home." The woman pushed her way into the house, keeping the gun pointed at Dee.

"I.. I .. Uh.. I don't have a roommate," Dee said.

"Then whoever it is that has that little dog," the woman said as she motioned the gun toward Bindi.

"I'm just dog sitting for a friend, they won't be back until the middle of next week." Dee tried to sound strong, but it came out as a whisper.

"You're the lady who saw Daryl in that house over there." Again, she waved the gun the direction she was referring to. "Don't think I don't know who you are. You sent your little stooge to find out who it was. And we caught her. Alex told me all about you. He and Daryl were watching your house to see if you'd call the cops and what do you know, they were here this morning. Stupid, stupid, stupid," the woman kept repeating as she walked around the house, the gun still aimed toward Dee.

"What do you want?" Dee asked.

"I want you to tell the cops you didn't see anyone in that

house, and I want you to convince your little friend you didn't see anyone either. And that she don't know who took her from the museum."

"I won't say anything, I promise," Dee slid into a chair next to the bay windows, spilling some of the whiskey that she was still carrying around.

"What's in your glass?" the woman asked.

"It's, um, it's whiskey."

The woman walked over and snatched the glass out of Dee's hand and upended the contents into her mouth.

"Get me another one," she said.

Dee stood and made her way into the kitchen and poured another drink. She drank it down, giving herself liquid courage, before filling the glass tumbler full, in the hopes of getting the woman drunk. It would allow her to escape, or maybe take the gun away? She shook her head, who was she kidding. She was in dire straits and needed to do whatever she could to get the woman out of her house.

She brought the glass, along with the bottle, back out and handed the glass to the woman. This time the woman took a small drink before motioning Dee back to the chair.

"You and I are going to wait together." The woman stood at the window watching the road. After another hour passed, a set of headlights came down the road. Again, a turn signal came on and the car turned into the driveway.

"They're going to ask about your car," Dee said, lifting her chin defiantly.

"And you're going to make up some story about it." The woman grabbed Lily by the collar and pulled her into a room off the kitchen. "I'll kill your dog if you make any mention of me being here, got it?"

Dee's eyes welled up with tears as she nodded.

Time stood still. Dee heard the ticking of the old grandfather clock, counting the seconds before Lorelei and the cops were at the door. Time stopped as she waited. A full minute passed before there was a slight knock and Dee heard the it open. She realized she hadn't lock it after the woman came in.

"Dee? Are you here?" Michael called out from downstairs.

"I'm up here." It came out as a whisper, she tried again, "I'm up here."

"I'm here, Dee," Lorelei called out.

Bindi jumped up from the couch and ran down the stairs to greet her person. Lorelei snatched her up and held Bindi close to her heart as she followed Michael and Amy up the stairs.

"I didn't think you were going to come in," Dee said nervously, looking at them then switching her gaze to the door the woman had gone through. She kept looking from the cops to the door, wide eyed. It was slightly ajar, but she couldn't see inside the room.

Michael gave a slight nod, acknowledging Dee's glances, as he stayed at the top of the steps. Lorelei ran into Dee's arms, with Amy following behind. Michael walked up next to Amy, who was in the middle of the front room.

"She's home safe and we have the men who took her. They are at the station. Michael and I have to get back to the station and take care of the paper work." She kept eye contact with both women and gave a slight nod.

Dee's eyes were still wide, but she nodded back and said, "I'll make sure to get some food in her, and I have a bed made up on the couch. She'll be staying with me tonight."

"We will call in the morning and check in. And give you both an update. You two should be able to rest easy tonight." Michael said as he and Amy headed back toward the stairs. They made it a point to be heard going down the stairs and leaving by slamming the door.

"Are you hungry?" Dee asked as she let go of Lorelei, then she saw movement at the top of the stairs again. It was both

Michael and Amy. He gave a slight wave to her, then put his finger to his lips. Dee stared at him, then looked at the room, and back at Michael. He nodded before he and his partner made their way over. The door faced the kitchen so the woman would not be able to see the cops against the wall.

"I could use some food. Hope you still have some of that pasta left." Lorelei said as she put Bindi down on the couch and turned to hug Dee again. She whispered something in her ear.

"Well, isn't this a sweet, yet short reunion," the woman said as she came out of the room, with the gun wavering between Dee and Lorelei.

Dee grabbed Lorelei and pushed her behind her, putting herself between Lorelei and the mad woman.

"I got more than one bullet, don't think I won't shoot you first to get to her," the woman started walking toward them.

"If there's going to be any shooting, I will be the one doing it," Michael's voice came from behind the woman. She whirled around and Michael knocked the gun from her hand as Amy rushed the woman and knocked her to the floor.

"Let me go!" the woman screamed as she kicked and bucked, trying to dislodge Amy from her back. Amy grabbed the woman's left wrist and pulled it back, securing it with handcuffs. She pulled until the woman's hand was between her shoulder blades. Amy then grabbed the right wrist and put the cuffs around the woman's other wrist. Amy stood and Michael helped her lift the large woman to her feet and turned her around. The woman was trying to pull away so Michael tightened his grip on the woman's shoulder.

"Cheri Hastings, you are under arrest," Amy said.

"I want a lawyer!" Cheri yelled in her face, "I want my phone call! You're gonna pay for this!"

"Screaming for a lawyer, just like your husband, get her out of here," Amy said to Michael as he led Cheri Hastings to the stairs.

Dee ran to the side room and swung open the door calling, "Lily, here girl!" as Lily ran out and jumped on Dee, almost knocking her over. As she hugged Lily, she asked Amy, "How did you know she was here?"

"We already had an APB for her car after Lorelei said there was a woman involved. She's married to the pawn shop owner. She'd already left so we were looking for her car. Didn't think she'd come here, though."

"She threatened to shoot Lily if I said anything to you when you got here." Dee's knees gave out as she collapsed to the floor next to the golden retriever, who put her head in Dee's lap.

"I'm sorry," Amy said.

"She wanted to make sure I wouldn't testify against the man I saw in Jim and Fran's house. And she wanted to make sure Lorelei would keep quiet, too." Dee looked down as she rubbed Lily's ears. "I think she was going to kill us," she continued, without looking up.

"You're safe now," Amy said, "both of you. Now get something to eat and something strong to drink, if you got it, and we will come by tomorrow."

"Do you know what time?" Lorelei asked.

"Not early," Amy said, "we still have work to do tonight and I, for one, plan on sleeping in." She stuck out her hand to Lorelei, but instead of shaking it, Lorelei hugged Amy Holloway.

"I don't know how to thank you," Lorelei said, choking back tears.

Amy gently hugged her back before pulling away. "I want to say we were just doing our jobs, but I am sure Michael will tell you something different. He was hell bent on finding you," she said.

"Can you thank him for me?" Lorelei asked.

"You can tell him yourself tomorrow. I'm sure you will be hearing from him soon."

Just then, Lorelei's phone went off. She dug in her purse and pulled it out. There was a message from Michael.

Don't scare me like that again.

Lorelei smiled as she read it. She texted back.

I'll try not to, but won't make any promises :)

"I think he's ready to go," Lorelei said.

"We'll be talking to you tomorrow," Amy said before turning to leave. Lorelei followed her down the stairs, thanked her again, then made sure the door was locked and the deadbolt set before heading back upstairs.

Dee was in the kitchen heating up the pasta. Lorelei noticed two small tumblers half-full with a golden liquid.

"I figured you could use that," Dee said as Lorelei picked up the tumbler closest to her. She grabbed the other and handed it to Dee, who was stirring the pan on the stove.

"I may need two, or even three," Lorelei said as she took a small drink.

"You and me, both." Dee tried to laugh but it came out as a sob. She could no longer hold back her tears.

Lorelei went to her, took the spoon out of her hand and set it on the counter before turning Dee to face her.

"I'm okay, I'm home safe," she said as she put her arms around Dee. Dee hugged Lorelei tightly for a moment then pulled back.

"Look at me, you'd think someone just told me my dog died..." Another sob escaped Dee.

"Lily is fine, Bindi is fine, and you are I are both here, and safe."

"I know," Dee said. Lorelei handed her a paper towel to wipe her eyes. Dee took it, wiped her face, then downed her glass of whiskey. She handed the empty glass to Lorelei, who had upended her own glass. "Fill them both back up, won't you?"

Lorelei refilled both glassed and took them, along with the bottle, to the table. She came back and got bowls and silverware. Dee followed her to the table with the pasta.

They sat and ate while Lorelei told Dee what had happened that day, and how she had seen the man at the museum. Dee let her speak, only interrupting occasionally to ask a question when she didn't understand something. When they finished eating, Dee took the left over food and the bowls back into the kitchen while Lorelei took the still two full tumblers to the front room where she waited for Dee.

They sat in silence as they watched the lights of a ship out on the ocean, the only thing visible in the night. Bindi curled on Lorelei's lap and Lily had her head resting in Dee's, enjoying the ear rub.

17

Lorelei was awaken by a cold nose nudging her chin. She rolled over, opened her eyes and saw sunshine and blue skies greeting her. She reached for her phone that sat on the coffee table next to the couch. The display read 10:45 am.

"Crap!" she said as she threw back the covers, "you must really need to go outside!" She sat up, rubbed the sleep from her eyes as her head throbbed from yesterday's excitement. The two tumblers of whiskey she and Dee finished hadn't help. She looked around and didn't see any sign of Dee. After making her way quietly down the stairs, she unlocked the door and let Bindi out, who ran across the yard to the back side, near the fence, and did her business.

Lorelei felt a bump on her backside and turned to see Lily, waiting patiently to go outside. She left the dogs outside to play in the sun as she made her way back upstairs and into the kitchen where she started the coffee and rummaged through the refrigerator looking for something to make for breakfast.

"I thought I would take you out for breakfast, well, now lunch," Dee said from behind her.

"That's thoughtful of you, but to tell you the truth, I would rather stay home. I don't care to be around people right now."

"I guess I can understand that," Dee said as she pulled two mugs from the drainer. She poured coffee as Lorelei continued looking through the fridge.

"How about an omelet?" Lorelei asked.

"That would be nice," Dee said.

"You go enjoy the view and I will make us breakfast."

Dee took her coffee and sat in her chair, facing the ocean. The storm had passed during the night and the sky was a crisp blue, but the ocean was still angry, with waves crashing on the large rocks out past the beaches. Today would be a better day. They could both relax, not worry about Jim and Fran's place, except to feed the cat, and hopefully, Dee thought, they would find the missing paintings.

"Do you want to eat in your chair or at the table?" Lorelei called out from the kitchen.

"The table," Dee said as she got up.

Lorelei had found mushrooms, avocados, and Swiss cheese to make the omelets. She had toast with marianberry jelly to go with it. They ate and talked about the last couple of days, wondering if they could have done anything different.

"I could have left it up to the police to find the man from the casino," Lorelei said, "but in a way I am glad I was able to find out who he was. And I had myself free from that back room before the police arrived. I would have been able to escape on my own. Time was on my side."

"It was still pretty risky," Dee said between mouthfuls, "and besides, you aren't trained like they are."

Before Lorelei could answer, her cell phone rang. She wiped her mouth and hands with her napkin and went to retrieve her phone. She looked at the number on the screen before she answered.

"Hello, Michael."

"How are you doing this morning?" he replied.

"I'm okay, better than I thought I would be, but I still have a bit of the adrenaline going through me," she said.

"I am wondering if you and Dee can come down to the station. I'd like to get statements from both of you, and go over what we already have."

Lorelei held the phone to her chest, "Dee, would you be up for a drive to the police station? They want us down there for official statements."

"I think so, when do they want us?" Dee said.

Lorelei put the phone back to her ear, "When do you want us there? And will I be able to get my car?"

"Whenever you have the time, my partner and I are here all day, and your car is still sitting behind the museum. We locked it back up after getting your dog out of it."

"Did you get any sleep?" Lorelei asked.

"No, we've been working all night," he said.

"Then we will be down as soon as we can, I don't want you waiting on us." Lorelei said.

"See you then," Michael said and hung up.

Lorelei finished her breakfast and took the plates into the kitchen. She rinsed them, and the bowls from last night, then put everything into the dishwasher. She wiped down the granite counter tops and made sure everything was put away before letting Dee know she was going home to shower and change her clothes.

She and Bindi went home. Lorelei unlocked the door to her little apartment, but she stopped before entering. She still felt apprehensive even though she knew the men who kidnapped her were in jail, along with that woman who showed up last night with a gun. Her heart beat heavy in her chest. Lorelei watched Bindi charge in and attack a stuffed toy, tossing it in the air and biting it to make is squeak, before she felt comfortable enough to enter. She took a deep breath, entered, then turned and locked the door behind her and put on the chain.

After her shower, she got dressed in Levi's and a soft sweater the color of mint. She went back into the bathroom and looked at herself. She didn't see the young, carefree woman who greeted her yesterday. The dark circles under her eyes, pale skin, and damp hair brought a well of tears to her eyes. She grabbed a towel and draped it over her shoulder before grabbing a pair of scissors and started cutting. Long, dark, red locks of hair fell to her feet as she continued to cut. By the time she was finished, much of her hair lay at her feet. When she finally looked in the mirror, her hair fell a few inches below her shoulders in dark ringlets. Without all the weight, her natural curls returned. She applied mousse before brushing it out. She found a few strands she missed, and cut them off as well. She draped the towel over the edge of the tub and went in search of a broom. Bindi followed her back into the bathroom, but Lorelei shooed her out. She looked down at the almost two feet of hair on the floor and carefully began picking it up, hoping she could donate it to Locks of Love. What she couldn't grab, she swept up and threw away.

Once the mess was cleaned up, she went to work hiding the trauma of yesterday that appeared on her face. She applied foundation to hide the dark circles under her eyes, applied eye liner and mascara, then dried her hair. When she had finished, she looked at the results. Her green eyes had life to them again, and she didn't feel as lost when she stared at her reflection. She hadn't done too bad a job on her hair. It was even, as far as she could tell. She pulled the front up out of her face and held it with a spider clip. She was ready to face Michael Smith and Amy Holloway to give her statement. She hadn't given one last night. They had taken her to the hospital to get checked out and when she was given the green light, they had taken her home.

She found her boots, pulled them on and called Bindi to

her.

"You have to stay home and protect the fort. I won't be gone long." She kissed Bindi's nose before locking up and making her way back to Dee's.

The look of surprise on Dee's face when she saw Lorelei's new look stopped Lorelei in her tracks.

"You don't like it?" She pulled at one of the curls and tucked it behind her ear.

"You were beautiful before, but now…" words escaped Dee.

"That bad?" Lorelei asked.

"It's gorgeous, it fits you," Dee laughed as she led Lorelei to the garage where Dee's Prius was parked.

They went to the museum first to retrieve Lorelei's car. It was as she left it yesterday, no worse for wear being left out in the storm last night. She got in and started it up then followed Dee to the police station a couple blocks away. Once there, they parked on the street and took the steps up to the City Hall building that housed the police station.

"We are here to see officers Smith and Holloway," Lorelei said to the woman at the counter.

"Let me get them for you," she said and disappeared through a side door. She returned a moment later and said, "Someone will be out to get you."

There were seats positioned against the walls in the small waiting room. They sat closest to the door that would lead them into the back of the police station. They didn't have long to wait before Amy Holloway came out.

"Thank you for coming down," she said. She did a double take at Lorelei before saying, "That's a good look for you."

"Thank you." Lorelei absent-mindedly reached up to her hair. It's amazing what cutting two feet from your hair can do for the psyche.

They followed Amy down a long hallway that opened up

into a large room filled with desks and a couple offices off the main floor. Most the desks were empty except two, where men in suits worked away. Amy led them around the desks and down another short hallway that had doors on either side. They made their way down to the end and entered the last door to their right. Inside, Michael sat at the large table with papers spread out in front of him. His blond hair stood up at odd angles, his uniform wrinkled from the long night of work. He looked up when the door opened and stared at Lorelei, unable to look away. She smiled at him as she entered, followed by Dee then Amy.

Suddenly, he got to his feet, "Thank you for coming, please have a seat." He motioned to the chairs across from him. He ran his fingers through his hair, creating more spikes. "Would you like some coffee?"

"If you don't mind," Dee answered as she took her seat.

"I'll have a cup too," Lorelei said as she sat in the chair to Dee's left, in front of Michael. Amy grabbed two cups, filled them, brought them over and set them down before taking a seat next to Michael, and across from Dee.

"I don't suppose you have anything to put in this," Dee said after taking a sip of the strong coffee.

"I'm sorry," Michael said. He leaned back in his chair and grabbed a basket of small creamers and some stir sticks from the counter behind him. He handed them to Dee who took them and placed them between herself and Lorelei. Both women put in enough creamer to change the color of the coffee.

"I have some pictures I need you to look at," Michael said to Dee as he handed her a small stack of photos.

She took them and looked at them, one at a time.

"This is one of the paintings taken from Jim and Fran's house," she said as she handed back in the photos. "I remember them telling me about their trip to Italy and their trip to wine country. They bought this as a reminder." She kept going through the photos but didn't recognize any more. "Are all these stolen?" she asked as she handed the rest back to Michael.

"We believe so. These were all in the back of the pawn shop."

At the mention of the back room, a chill ran down Lorelei's spin. Her face paled as she tried to hide the fear in her eyes. Michael caught this and wanted to jump over the table and take her in his arms and hold her close. Instead, he held her gaze for a moment, then a moment longer, until he noticed her color coming back. He looked back at the photos he was still holding.

"We had officers at the pawn shop all night, taking pictures of the inventory. We will be contacting the families who reported burglaries in the last three months. Hopefully we can get the pieces back to their rightful owners. We don't know how many have already been sold but we will be tracking those down too."

"For those of us who paid for the stolen artwork, will we be reimbursed?" Lorelei asked.

"We are hoping that we can find all the buyers," Amy cut in, "and get the pieces back. If they paid cash, we have no way of knowing where the pieces went. But with the kind of prices he was asking, there would be a paper trail, if they paid by credit card, like you did."

"We found a receipt with your name on it," Michael said before Lorelei could ask the question.

"I can just call the credit card company and cancel the purchase. And if need be get a copy of the police report," Lorelei said matter of factly.

This brought a smile to Michael's tired face.

"Then let's get to that paperwork," Amy said as she pulled out a notebook from under the scattered papers, "so we can all get home soon. I, for one, am in need of a shower and sleep."

Michael interviewed Dee at one end of the table, while Amy interviewed Lorelei at the other end, keeping the two separate while they answered questions. The two officers wanted to make sure it was done properly so nothing would come back on them if this went to court. It took a couple hours before both Michael Smith and Amy Holloway were satisfied that they had covered everything.

"I want to thank you for your time, and your help," Amy said as she and Lorelei stood. Michael had finished up with Dee fifteen minutes before and had taken her out of the room.

"Can I go home now?" Lorelei asked.

"Yes, I think we have everything. They've all lawyered up so we haven't been able to talk to them. I'm hoping they will take a plea deal since they are all being charged with kidnapping and attempted murder, along with the burglaries." Amy opened the door for Lorelei and walked her down the hallway. Lorelei didn't see Dee anywhere.

"Did Dee leave?" she asked.

"She's in the ladies room," Michael answered from behind her.

Startled, she turned and found herself so close she could feel the heat from his body.

"Thank you, I just didn't want to leave without her."

"Can I talk to you?" Michael asked, "outside, before you head home?"

"Sure," she said, then turned to Amy, "Can you let Dee know I'll be outside waiting for her?"

"I can do that," Amy said as a smile spread across her face, showing her perfect teeth.

Michael held Lorelei's elbow as he escorted her out of the building and to her car. Lorelei leaned against the driver's door as Michael stood close in front of her.

"I was wondering, when this is all over, would you mind if I called you and took you to dinner?" he asked as he took her hands.

"What do you mean, when this is all over?" she asked, intertwining her fingers with his.

"With this being an open case, and now that Amy and I are part of the investigation, I need to keep this as professional as I can. It wouldn't look good if I was dating the main witness."

"How long do I have to wait? I mean, I do have things to do, people to see, and places to go," she said giving him her best smile.

"With everything we have, I don't think you'll have to forgo your plans for too long." He pulled her close and gently kissed her cheek before whispering in her ear, "You are the most beautiful woman I've met in a very long time."

She pulled back, smiled, and said, "I think I can handle that. Can we talk while we wait for that dinner?"

"I honestly don't know. I will talk it over with my partner, since this will affect her too." Michael kept his arms draped on her shoulders.

"I don't want to jeopardize anything for either of you. I can wait. I still have to find a job and am going to have to find someone to help me remodel my house. I'm not going anywhere." She stood on tip toes and kissed his cheek. "Dee's coming, and I'm sure you're ready to go home and get some sleep."

"I am," he said, "and I will be in touch, one way or another." He leaned back over but instead of her cheek, his let his lips softly press against hers before he turned to leave.

18

"I know what I want to do," Lorelei said a week later, while she was having lunch with Dee at Miller's, the sports bar in Charleston.

"What's that?" Dee asked.

"I going to be a Private Detective," she said.

"A what?" Dee spit her coffee out, almost spraying Lorelei.

"No, really," Lorelei laughed, "I've been giving it some thought. I did pretty well at finding the man who broke into the house, and the stolen art work."

"And you got yourself kidnapped!" Dee reminded her.

Lorelei took a bite of her grilled fish taco before continuing, "But I also escaped, you keep forgetting that part. And, I found the perfect way to do this. I found this detective course online. I've ordered the text books, and bought a new camera. I figure I can work for one of the insurance companies here in town as an official photographer or something, taking pictures of claims and what not, and study the courses in the evening."

"You're crazy!" Dee said as she wiped up the coffee. "What do you know about being a detective?"

"Nothing, that's why I'm taking the course, but being a

photographer is something I'm good at. I've already been in touch with an insurance company here in town. I showed them my skills and I start next Monday. So I have this week to get everything in order before I start my new adventure. I can't keep living off what Mom gives me every month. I have to make my own way."

Dee nodded

"Want to see my new home, across from you. I haven't taken you there yet, have I?"

"Actually, no, you haven't, but that's no fault of yours, we've been too busy every time you brought it up."

"Let me give you a tour," Lorelei said.

"Let's go," Dee laughed and finished her coffee.

Back at Dee's, they leashed the dogs and went across the street. The house had an unobstructed view of the Pacific Ocean. The detached garage was newly built and had a small office, which Lorelei loved, that faced the ocean. The small house had a large cedar deck that went clear to the bluffs. Most of the boards were new and those that needed replacing were few and far between. The railing around the deck was also new, so there was one less thing to worry about. Lorelei escorted Dee into the main living area, which was pretty much the main floor. There were two rooms off to the right, where the bedroom and bathroom were located. The walls needed painted, the floor needed to be stripped and refinished, but other than that, Lorelei was home.

Once inside, they let the dogs run. Bindi sniffed every corner, checking out the new place. Lily stood in the middle of the main room, watching her, not sure if she wanted to leave Dee's side.

"My plan is to have the bathroom redone, made larger to add a laundry room, instead of having the washer and dryer off the back porch. And I'll add a loft that will be the master bedroom. I'll keep the other bedroom for a guest room when I have company. But I want to open this place up, have the entire west wall windows, so I have an unobstructed view of the light house and the ocean," Lorelei started, and took Dee on a tour showing her all the things she had planned.

Dee and Lorelei headed back to Dee's house.

"I finally have a home of my own!" Lorelei exclaimed.

"Yes, you do," said Dee as looked for cars before crossing the road.

"I hate the way I got it, but I am so thrilled to be back home," Lorelei sobered for a moment, but was caught up in the excitement again. "I need to find a contractor who will get this done for me."

"I can get you the number for the contractor Harry and I used, when we had the house build. And Lorelei," Dee stopped and turned to face her, "I understand your excitement. We had insurance on our mortgage. So when I lost Harry, our home was paid off. I hated losing him, but he was able to offer me security, knowing he wouldn't be around to help me. It's kind of the same here."

Lorelei tucked her arm into Dee's as they started up Dee's driveway.

The mailman was unloading a large box from his jeep. He walked over and placed it next to Dee's gate. Lorelei had to tighten her grip on Bindi's leash. After she passed him, she tucked Bindi behind the gate before turning back.

"Can I get that for you?" Lorelei asked.

"Are you Lorelei Silence?" he asked.

"I am."

"I need you to sign for these, please." He set the box down by the gate and pulled out an electronic gadget for her to sign. As she signed for the package, he pulled out another box the same size, from his vehicle, and set it next to the first. She thanked him as she handed back his electronics.

"Don't forget your mail," he called to her. She followed him to his jeep and grabbed their mail. She handed Dee her's and went through her own. She had a couple envelopes address to occupant, but her cheeks reddened as she noticed the writing on one of the envelopes. It was a card from Michael.

"Is that from your cop friend?" Dee asked her when she saw the smile grow across Lorelei's face.

"It is," she grinned, "but we can't talk until this case is closed. Wonder what it is?" She opened the card. It was a silly card, with a dog on the front running from the photographer. The inside was blank except for a few words written. She read, "Don't forget we have a dinner date when all this ends, Michael."

She smiled as she returned the card to the envelope. She walked over to the boxes by the gate. The return address label read "Acme Private Investigators".

"Oh my gosh! This day keeps getting better and better!"

Printed in Great Britain
by Amazon